The Red Shark

OTHER BOOKS ABOUT HAWAII BY
RUTH TABRAH

EMILY'S HAWAII
NI'IHAU, THE LAST HAWAIIAN ISLAND
THE GOLDEN CHILDREN OF HAWAII
KAUA'I: THE UNCONQUERABLE ISLAND
HAWAII'S INCREDIBLE ANNA
MAUI: THE ROMANTIC ISLAND
HAWAII: A HISTORY
LANAI
HAWAII NEI

The Red Shark

Ruth M. Tabrah

COVER AND ILLUSTRATIONS BY
PAT HALL

Press Pacifica

Library of Congress Cataloging-in-Publication Data

Tabrah, Ruth M., 1921-
    The red shark.

        Summary: When his father moves the family
from Chicago back to the island of Hawaii, a ninth grade
boy finds mystery, suspense, and a respect for the
old-time spirit of the island.
        [1. Hawaii Island (Hawaii)—Fiction]   I. Hall,
Pat, ill. II. Title.
PZ7.T115Re 1989   [Fic]   89-23109
ISBN 0-916630-67-6

© Ruth M. Tabrah 1970

Printed at Thomson-Shore, Inc., Dexter, Michigan

Available from Press Pacifica,
P.O. Box 47, Kailua, Hawaii 96734
(808) 261-6594

ISBN 0-916630-67-6

THIS STORY COULD not have been written without the inspiration and encouragement of Henry Doi of Kawaihae who spent his life in a place like Wainalii. I owe a debt of deepest gratitude as well to Heloke Mookini of North Kohala who shared with me the legends of his deep rooted Hawaiian-ness. And I must not forget to thank my Kawaihae friend Eddie Kealanahele, who was always going to take me out swimming to meet his shark friend.

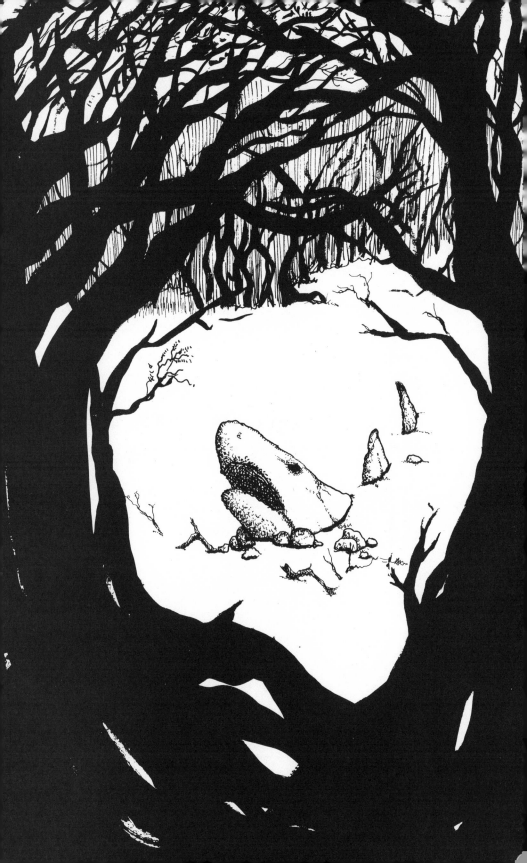

CHAPTER ONE

It was strange waking at dawn on a beach on an island in the middle of the Pacific Ocean.

Stanley Sasaki, a shy, skinny boy with black hair that kept falling down over his eyes, was five thousand miles away from home. Nothing on this remote part of the Big Island looked, or felt, or sounded like anywhere else he had been. It was the first night he had slept on a grass mat on a beach. His first night spent with the threatening sound of surf rolling in long crescendoes against the reef. His first look at this place. His father had brought him along to help decide if they should move over here.

Stanley threw off his blanket and sat up.

His father lay snoring on his grass mat, his

blanket wrapped around him like a cocoon against the mosquitoes that had attacked them during the night.

The park where they were camped had an even lonelier, more deserted air about it this morning than when they'd driven in at dusk last night. The village, separated from the park by a low lava stone wall, was a cluster of silent houses in the gray dawn light. Not a rooster had crowed. No pig yet stirred. No dog had roused to bark.

Stanley whispered the name of the place. "Wainalii." It was a strange sounding name to his Chicago ears.

He turned, with a stir of impulse, to look in the other direction. Yes, there it was. The trail pierced the barricade of thorny trees at the far end of the beach. It had been the first thing Stanley noticed last night. Something about it seemed to tempt his feet, and his curiosity. He had even dreamed about it.

Careful not to make a sound to disturb his father, Stanley stood up. He had slept in his jeans and T-shirt. He could follow the trail now—while his dad slept. Stanley hesitated. He had left his sneakers in the station wagon, loaned them by one of his father's Hilo cousins.

I'll go barefoot, like they do around here, he decided. He didn't want to risk waking his father. Alone, that's how he wanted to explore the trail.

10

The first few steps across the beach the sand was comfortable under his shoe-accustomed feet. Then he entered the narrow trail. Sharp stones poked into his tender soles. He stubbed his toe on a thorny downfall. He slowed, picking each step with care. The branches closed in around the trail, catching on his T-shirt and raking his face and neck and bare arms. It did not look as if it had much use.

After a minute or two, when Stanley turned to look back, he could see nothing but the thorny green wall of foliage closing in around the narrow curving tunnel of the trail. No glimpse of the beach. No sign of the palm grove and the village. No sound except his own breathing, the creak of tree branches, the long slow surge of surf on the reef that guarded Wainalii Bay. He was tempted to turn back. It was a queer feeling to be so alone, so far away from anything or anyone. He looked ahead. A trail always led someplace. Stanley shivered. He had the odd sensation that whether he wanted to turn back or not didn't matter. Something seemed to pull at his feet to continue on.

A half mile further, the trail emerged from the trees at a rock point. Wainalii lay hidden behind him in its deep bay, screened by the jungle through which the trail had led him on to this next, smaller bay. The barren, gulch-gouged slopes of the island's interior loomed above him. The coastline south stretched out in a series of desolate bays and points and lava flows that descended from a long blue mountain with no sign of any building or road on its flanks. The pale sky, the flat steely ocean, were so immense that Stanley, unused to being able to see such distances, felt uneasy. On the horizon, the neighboring island of Maui floated in a vague blue silhouette. Stanley shivered again. It was like being on a desert island.

Across a shallow cove, Stanley could see the trail piercing on into another jungle of thorny, tangled trees. The sun would be up soon. He ought to turn back now, but his feet still felt the urge to keep on. He waded into the shallow water. Tiny silver and yellow fish startled out of his way. Every detail of stones and sand and chunks of dead coral on the bottom glimmered through the transparent water. "Wow!" Stanley exclaimed aloud. This was not like the water he was used to in Lake Michigan.

Anyone following the trail would choose to wade directly across the cove in a shortcut to it. Stanley's first impulse was to do this. Then he took a second look at the lip of white sand edging the cove. It was not much of a beach, but he wanted to go stand on it. It was such a small, perfect, empty crescent of sand. The fresh skittery tracks of a bird and a gaping crab hole marked one edge. The tracing of debris from high tide was washed in an uneven series of scallops up under the branches of the trees that grew down to the sand. To Stanley, it was a beach that looked and felt as if no one else had ever been here before.

He detoured toward it, out of the shallow water. He patterned the prints of his bare feet along the bird tracks. He paused, staring at something that caught his attention along the high-tide mark. He was not sure, even when he went up and looked closely, whether it was maybe a place some animal might have used to get down to the beach or the entrance to another faint trail that caught his eye.

The path—if that's what it was—was only a hint through the litter of tide-washed coconut husks and lumps of broken coral and bleached dead shells. And more than the first trail leading here from Wainalii, this faint trace of path felt like a magnet for his feet. He explored cautiously under the low branches.

"Ouch!" A thorn stuck in his heel. He balanced on the other foot and yanked it out. He continued on, limping. The light under the trees was dim. He had to bend double to crouch beneath the branches. Every few steps inland he stopped, and looked all around, and listened. The sound of the ocean kept him sure he knew at least that direction. From the lack of choice in ways for his feet to go, Stanley could tell that something or someone had used this path to get in and out from the beach.

He had groped a good hundred feet when light opened ahead. He stepped out from the last low branch into a clearing where he could stand erect.

"Oh!"

One look and he retreated so fast a thorn gouged blood from his cheek. A branch caught and ripped his T-shirt. Stanley's mouth opened. No sound would come out. In a panic, he tore the branch loose from his shirt. His heart was pounding the wild rate of fear. It took all his courage not to turn and run.

In the middle of the clearing, lying on its belly, facing him, was what looked like a great black shark. It was a boulder, the size and shape of a shark. There was a bulge on its back that looked like a shark's fin. Two deep pockmarks looked out from the stone head like shark eyes. The mouth was an evil underslung curve.

The peculiar dawn light, the quiet, the sense of being so far away in a strange place, all added to Stanley's overwhelming certainty. The shark-shaped stone was not lying here as any ordinary stone might. There was an eerie quality about it, an eerie atmosphere in this clearing. What it was, Stanley had no idea. Whatever it might be, he knew without knowing how he knew that he was not supposed to be in here. There was a feeling of presence in the stone. It was not logical to be afraid of it. Yet, he was!

"It's the light," Stanley said aloud, hopefully.

The stone seemed to listen. The small alert stone eyes gazed back at him. The longer Stanley looked and stood there, the more powerful the illusion became.

A branch creaked nearby with an odd moaning sound.

Stanley turned. The stone eyes followed him.

"No. Don't!" Stanley pleaded. Not caring how badly the thorns might rake him, he bolted out through the trees, onto the narrow crescent of the tiny beach, out into the shallow water of the cove, back onto the trail and along it as fast as he could go to the grass mats and his father on the beach at Wainalii.

CHAPTER TWO

It felt like forever to Stanley before his dad woke up. He didn't intend to tell where he had been or what he had seen. There was too lingering a sense of the forbidden about that strange shark-shaped stone. All Stanley wanted was the reassurance of his dad's comfortable, eager talk about the morning, and breakfast, the weather, and all the pros-and-cons of settling in Wainalii, where they had inherited Uncle Kenji's six acres, house, and store.

Ichiro Sasaki was a short, slightly built man with a pleasant round face and graying hair. His shoulders were stooped from having worked in a post office the years since he'd been a teenager in the all-Nisei island regiment that fought its way to fame in World War

II. Stanley's mother was mainland born and raised. She, Stanley speculated, would not believe a place like Wainalii could be. Stanley sighed. He could not stand feeling so alone. He began lobbing small chunks of coral into the sand. That roused his dad.

"Eh, Stanley! You up already!" Mr. Sasaki stretched, yawned, sat up and started to grin a good morning. One look at Stanley's face and his expression changed. Abashed, Stanley tried to rub the dried blood from his cheek. "Ouch!" he said, starting the bleeding again.

"What happened to you?" Mr. Sasaki looked worried. "And your shirt's torn too."

"I went for a walk before you got up," said Stanley. "Those crazy trees over there are full of thorns." He started to revive last night's fire. Anything to avert his scratched face from his father's questioning eyes.

"Ah. There's so much I have to tell you about this place, Stanley! Like, be careful when you walk in a kiawe forest. Those thorns, they're so sharp they can poke through slipper soles."

"Ummmm." Stanley reached surreptitiously for his sore heel. "Kiawes?" he repeated. Even the trees had different names over here. He was amazed how his father used different words, had a different way of speaking since they got off the plane in Hilo day before yesterday. "Pidgin," explained Stanley's cousins whom he was seeing for the first time and who spoke the same odd-sounding dialect. It might be English, Stanley thought, but to him it didn't sound like any English he'd heard before.

He gave up on the dead coals and built a new fire in the park grill to cook their breakfast eggs and sausages. When they finished eating, Stanley went down to wash the plates and the frying pan in the edge of the bay. He did as his father had shown him last night, scouring the grease with a handful of sand and alternately rubbing and rinsing until the tin plates and frying pan loaned by Aunt Hatsu were clean.

"First thing they have to do when they develop this place is run water down from the mountain," said Mr. Sasaki. "You see the wooden tanks by each house and the way the roof drains rainwater into the tank? That's how Wainalii gets its drinking water. The pipes you see, that's only for bathing and laundry. From a brackish well. Too salty to use for drinking unless sometimes you have to when there's a drought."

Stanley washed his face and hands in the brackish water from the faucet in the park. He combed through his hair with his damp fingers and put on a fresh T-shirt from his suitcase in the back of the station wagon. He banged open the door and started to get into the front seat of the station wagon.

"Stanley. Where do you think you're going?"

Stanley poised halfway into the seat, one foot still on the road. "Up to look at Uncle Kenji's place," he said.

"Not in the car, though." Mr. Sasaki shook his head. "You forget how to use your feet Stanley? Over here, no need use a car to go every place. No sense." And he started off up the road through Wainalii village.

Stanley banged the door shut, but stood beside the station wagon. "Hey, Dad! You want me to bring the keys—only no way to lock this car too good—"

"No need to lock up. No need to bring the keys," said Mr. Sasaki, waiting for him.

Stanley still hesitated. All their gear in the open back of the station wagon. His suitcase with his new clothes for the trip. The transistor radio he had won in a contest for newscarriers. In Chicago, any car left like that was stolen clean and gone before you were a block away.

"No worries! Nobody will take anything." His father spoke with an assurance Stanley could not share. He began walking behind his dad, but his feet were reluctant. Mr. Sasaki looked all around with pleasure. Stanley had no desire to gaze at the village houses built up on their high stilts of foundation posts, at the morning shadow pattern of the palm grove dappling the tin roofs. He took only an occasional glance ahead at the blacktop road leading on past the coral surfaced turn-off into the palm grove, on past the steep driveway that led to Uncle Kenji's store and property, past the abandoned shack that had been the post office, to a dead end at the ruins of a pier. He kept looking instead back over his shoulder to keep a wary eye on the station wagon. He wondered if the kids passing them on the way to the one-room school beyond the park were as easy about snitching things as a lot of the kids he went to school with.

Mr. Sasaki had been born in Hilo, ninety miles away on the windward side of the island. After his father died, he had spent his summers in Wainalii with Uncle Kenji and his Hawaiian wife, who had no children of their own.

"Wainalii hasn't changed. Not since I was your age," Mr. Sasaki reminisced. He waved to a man passing in an open jeep.

"You remember him?" asked Stanley.

"Let's see—Yama Ching, maybe." Mr. Sasaki shrugged. "Hard to remember the names after so long. Once, though, I knew everybody in Wainalii. Good feeling to live where you know everybody and everybody knows you. I'd like for you and your sisters to grow up in a place where you can be like that . . . and where you don't have to be afraid."

20

At the driveway to the store, Stanley could no longer see around the long curve in the road and back to the station wagon. He hesitated, still uneasy, and then followed his father up for the first daylight look at their inheritance. Last night it had been impossible to tell about things by flashlight, except that the place had looked too dirty and abandoned to sleep in. That was why they had camped in the park. To Stanley, nothing about the property had looked too promising in the flashlight's beam.

"Terrific, no?" exclaimed Mr. Sasaki with an enthusiasm that baffled Stanley. "This place has real potential, I tell you!"

Stanley wondered if anything could have happened in the last two days to his father's eyesight. The store building seemed ready to fall down. Several small sheds were in no better shape. Neither was the house. All the doors and windows were boarded up with scrap lumber and pieces of corrugated roofing tin. The store porch sagged at one end. Sections of tin roof were rusted through. There were broken windowpanes where rats and mongooses had gotten inside. The foundation posts were honeycombed with the holes of termites and carpenter bees.

"Nice tree," said Stanley, looking up at the big milo that shaded the courtyard in front of the store. "And you can sure see all over from up here." There was nothing else he could see that looked encouraging.

"I knew you'd like it!" said Mr. Sasaki.

Stanley turned away, embarrassed by his father's pleasure at what he'd said. "How come," Stanley asked, "if nobody steals anything around here, that they had to padlock the doors and board up all the windows?"

Mr. Sasaki laughed. "Still worrying about the car? That's different, Stanley. Like with these old buildings, if nobody's around a long time, and it doesn't look like anybody's going to make use of them again, people might come help themselves to whatever's around. The boarding up and the padlock, that's a signal for kapu. Don't touch or take anything. Somebody owns it still. Too bad it's all different now I hear in Honolulu. Stealing. All the time stealing. But not in this kind of village. Not on this island. Our leaving the car open, that's the signal we're strangers who trust the people of Wainalii."

"Ummm," said Stanley. He wondered if Wainalli might not have changed in the years since his father spent summers here. Silently he followed from store to house to shed to bathhouse to another shed. They unlocked padlocks. They tested rotten places in the floors. Spider webs caught in Stanley's face. Wasps cruised menacingly in and out of their mud nests.

22

"Watch out! Scorpion!" His dad pulled Stanley back from a three-inch-long scorpion poised with tail curled over his back ready to sting.

Until noon they looked through the buildings. They walked the stone-wall boundaries of the six acres. They sat on a ramshackle bench under the milo tree looking at the view. Stanley stared down at the village houses, tranquil in the noon heat. It was nothing like a Chicago November day. In the palm grove that cloistered the fifty-odd houses, people sat in the shade mending fishing nets, or strumming ukuleles, or lazily doing nothing. In the shallows at the edge of the bay, women squatted picking and eating something, their skirts draped up around their thighs and dangling in the water. Between the houses, lean pigs rooted at piles of split coconuts. A man worked on his outrigger canoe. A dog lay sleeping in the middle of the road.

Stanley glanced down at the kiawe jungle that lay south of the park. Even from this height the trees hid any glimpse of the hidden cove or the clearing where the shark-shaped stone lay. "Dad—" Stanley cleared his throat, despite the queer conviction he had that he ought not to mention to anyone, even his Dad, what he had seen. "This morning . . ."

His father, preoccupied with his own thoughts,

didn't hear him. "Eh, Stanley!" he exclaimed, with an expansive fling of his arms that embraced all that surrounded them. "This is it! Our chance! Our lucky break! Six acres fee simple. Left to us. You understand, Stanley? Before, maybe this land was worth nothing in Wainalii. Now, it's different. Millions of tourists coming to the islands every year. New hotels going up all over I tell you, there's no limit to the future for Wainalii! This climate? You can't beat it! The scenery? Take a look! Atmosphere, real atmosphere. That's the pull to this place. Something different. Like a tropical beach village looks in the movies you see. A real paradise!

"And we can live here. We have six acres fee simple. Fee simple, Stanley! You don't know what that is for the islands. Not easy to buy land in Hawaii, now or ever. The big companies, the state government, the kamaaina rich families, they're the ones own most of everything. They won't sell. Not one house lot. They only lease the land to you. Cousin Kenneth, you know his house where we stayed in Hilo? He only has a fifty-year lease on the ground his house is on. Once the lease is up, his house and all the improvements he made–they go back to the company owns the land. Every year he has to pay ground rent. Plus the taxes, and that ground rent is high. It costs him plenty every year, but no matter how he has tried to buy–they won't sell to him.

"Uncle Kenji's wife, this was her family land, passed down from the days Hawaii was a kingdom eighty years ago. Fee simple. Ours, that's what that means! I think they knew how I felt for Wainalii, how always I dreamed of being able to come back here someday. The best part of my life was when I was young spending those summers here. All the things I did then, I want for you and your sisters to have the chance to do too. The chance to grow up where you know everybody, where you can walk anyplace, where you don't have to be afraid of anything–" Mr. Sasaki looked with nostalgia down at the village. "And where things don't change, Stanley. This is one place, here, where nobody tears the old buildings down and puts more and more big new ones up. Atmosphere. That's the potential!" He stood up so abruptly that Stanley was almost catapulted from his end of the bench.

"What you think, Stanley? We crazy, we don't take the chance we have now to move over here?"

Stanley hesitated. He wished he could see back to the unlocked car. He wished he knew what that shark stone in the clearing was. He wished he knew somebody–anybody here. And to make a living from running a store in this small a place?

"This is why I brought you, Stanley. To help me make up my mind. Now you see it—you don't feel bad to leave your school and your friends and your paper route, and the Y—to come live over here?"

Stanley swallowed. How could he say anything but what he knew his dad wanted him to! He tried to sound convinced. "It'd be great living here— really, I think—" He hated to lie, even when he knew he had to. His father's delighted grin, and the affectionate grip of his father's arm across his shoulders made him feel like a hypocrite.

"I knew it, Stanley! I knew you'd think like me!" He started off, almost at a run, down the steep drive. "This afternoon," he decided, "we'll go fix up the papers with the lawyer in Hilo. Tomorrow we'll look for a used truck. I'll get Uncle Arthur to check on the post office appointment with his political friends —it's supposed to be a sure thing for me if I want it. Ah, Stanley, the good life for us here! I hate to go back to Chicago even for one day."

Stanley had to hurry to keep up with his father.

"Wait till your mother sees Wainalii. Wait till we tell her, Stanley! I'm counting on you to help make her want to come over here!"

His mother? Stanley tried but could not imagine her in Wainalii.

When they reached the station wagon, everything was exactly as they had left it. The key was in the ignition. The suitcases and carton of food and sleeping mats were in back. Stanley opened his suitcase and got out his transistor radio and turned it on. He grinned with relief. "Wow!" he said. "This is someplace different! Nobody swiped a thing!"

CHAPTER THREE

The next time Stanley woke at dawn on the beach in Wainalii they were here to stay. His mother, his two small sisters, his grandmother Ba-chan, were waiting in Hilo with relatives until he and his father got the house ready for them.

Stanley had no urge to explore this morning. The memory of the shark stone was still vivid in his mind after two months. He shuddered now, as he looked at the trail. He'd had nightmares about that stone.

Stanley turned his head, propped himself on an elbow, and looked instead at the secondhand panel truck lettered "I. Sasaki and Son." His mental image of the stone was superimposed on the blue lettering.

"And Son," Stanley read it with determination, and awe. No use. He could not stop thinking about the stone and wondering whether, if he did go back up that faint trail, it would still be there looking back at him with its shark eyes.

"Stanley!" said his father.

Stanley jumped, and then felt foolish. "Oh," he said. "Good morning, Dad."

While they cooked and ate breakfast, the sun came up. A man in jeans, black leather jacket, and boots came out from one of the houses of the village. "Yama Ching, I bet you!" said Mr. Sasaki.

Yama Ching's unmuffled jeep motor roused all the dogs and roosters and brought a man out to the verandah of the nearest, and largest, of the village houses.

"Look at the big bugger! Six foot six, you think? And easy three hundred pounds! That's what you call a real Kamehameha, that big Hawaiian there."

Stanley gazed with respect at the great belly thrust into the morning air between a too short gray sweat shirt and a pair of low-riding khaki shorts. "Big!" he agreed.

As they watched, the man walked with slow dignity down the steps from his house and into a palm-thatched lean-to that served as garage. He came out carrying an outboard motor in one hand and a six-gallon gas can in the other.

Along the village area of the beach was a row of outrigger canoes. They were pulled up on the sand beyond reach of the highest tide. Each was shielded with scraps of roofing tin weighted with stones. Each was painted a different color—orange, green, red, brilliant blue, yellow. One, longer and narrower, different in shape from the others, was varnished black, with bright yellow gunwhales and a rubbed natural finish on the outriggers.

The big Hawaiian walked over to the black canoe. He set the motor and gas can down. He took off the stones and propped the roof tins against the trunk of a coconut palm. Stanley and his father were no more than fifty feet away, but the man never looked at them. He made a trip back to his house-yard for an armload of opelu nets. He made a second trip for a washtub, a box of oatmeal, and a bucket of something. From the bucket, the overripe garbage smell of rotten papaya, fermented cooked sweet potatoes, meat scraps, and avocado came so power-fully to Stanley's nose that he pushed back his break-fast plate.

"Hauna." Mr. Sasaki made a wry face. "Plenty strong bait by the smell!"

The man loaded the hauna bucket and nets and all the other things into the canoe. He fastened the motor on the transom. He took a pair of long poles wrapped in a furl of yellow canvas and stepped one pole as a mast.

"Stanley! That's a sailing canoe!" Mr. Sasaki got up and walked to the beach for a closer look. Stanley followed. His dad walked over, introduced himself, and shook hands. The Hawaiian returned the handshake, gave a somber nod to Stanley, but did not introduce himself to them.

"A sailing canoe! I thought there weren't any more around for years now!" said Mr. Sasaki. "She really does sail?"

"Sure."

Stanley touched the varnished black hull. It felt like glass. He took his hand from the canoe and stepped back, wondering if he shouldn't have touched the varnish. The Hawaiian gave him a quick strange glance. Then he stepped quickly between hull and outriggers to drag the canoe to the water.

"Here! We'll help!" said Mr. Sasaki.

The canoe was in the water before either of them had time to lend a hand. They stood, watching him paddle out.

Stanley turned at a burst of noise from the big Hawaiian's house. A woman was standing on the porch combing her waist-length hair. A man stood talking to her, cradling a rooster in the crook of his arm. He bent, tethering the rooster to a stake in the

31

ground. "What language are they talking back there?" Stanley asked his dad.

Mr. Sasaki listened. "English," he said, looking with astonishment at Stanley. "Pidgin English. You don't understand them? The old man sounds like a Filipino, maybe the Filipino accent fools your ear."

Stanley kept listening. He still couldn't get more than a stray word. He sighed. Some of the things his father said, and his Hilo cousins, were hard for him to understand.

As soon as he tethered the rooster, the Filipino came down on the beach and stood next to Stanley, looking at him and his dad with open curiosity.

In the black canoe, the paddle dipped in and out of the water with a steady rhythm, carrying the canoe along parallel with the beach toward the abandoned pier.

"Come! We see more better up the beach!" urged the Filipino. He jogged in the direction of the canoe.

"More better," Stanley repeated to himself as he followed the two men. Everybody was excited about hoisting a sail, which Stanley had seen done more times than he could remember on summer Sundays when they went to the park at Lake Michigan. "More better," he repeated under his breath.

Alongside the derelict pier the paddler backwatered. He drifted out past the sea-eaten concrete pilings. At the end of the pier, he lifted the paddle and whacked the flat side of the blade against the water three times. The noise was like three rifle shots echoing across the bay. *Whack! Crack! Whack!*

"Eh." The Filipino sucked in his breath and pointed. "Look!"

A long dark shadow moved out from beneath the pier at the noise of the signal. A fin glinted above the water's sunstruck surface. Stanley strained to see, feeling the same queer prickling sensation as when he'd seen the shark stone.

"Isaac's pet. He lead Isaac out everytime to the opelu school." The Filipino sounded proud.

"A shark?" Mr. Sasaki shaded his eyes with his hand to see better. The dark shadowy shape was, Stanley judged, at least six feet long.

"No shark that one. Barracuda—kaku. Isaac's pet. He fish with Isaac for maybe ten years now like this. When the opelu are running, he lead Isaac out to them. He stay hiding while Isaac chum with the hauna. When the opelu come up for eat, the kaku comes back, scares all the opelu into Isaac's net. That's why Isaac comes home every time from fishing with his washtub full. Two, three times a week he goes to Hilo with a truckload of fish. Dry opelu. The Hilo markets pay big money for Isaac's one because his kind dry opelu, it's the best."

Stanley watched the barracuda swimming toward the canoe. As it neared, the man started his outboard. He steered for the pass in the reef that guarded Wainalii Bay. The barracuda followed him out to sea as, on land, a dog might follow his master's car.

"Isaac? Isaac Kaimana?" his father said in an uneasy voice. His eyes, like Stanley's, were fixed on the long dark shadow swimming behind the canoe. "I heard about Isaac Kaimana. Only he was gone from Wainalii the summers I was here. My uncle talked plenty about him. Everybody did. He's strong Hawaiian, that Isaac Kaimana. Plenty akamai."

The Filipino nodded. "Isaac, he knows all the kind! Every fish in the ocean. Every cloud what it means in the sky. All the old Hawaiian kind things. Even, he no scare the shark! He can talk to the shark. He tell me so, and I believe. Ah—" He looked with pride at the canoe. The motor sound stopped. The yellow sail unfurled and bellied.

A man who could talk to sharks? Stanley looked apprehensively back at the kiawe jungle and the trail that led toward the shark-stone clearing. Issac Kaimana, he guessed, was the one who knew all about that, too.

"You stop this place before?" The Filipino asked Mr. Sasaki. "Somebody tell to me, one relative of old man Sasaki going move over open up the store.

You?'' There was a gleam of recognition, a big grin. "Ichiro? No! Cannot be! You came old too fast. You no remember me, Ichiro? Mateo Palabang. The one had the sampan then. My boat, my compang Benny Toledo, they both get smashed up in the big tidal wave. Now, no boat. No compang. No nothing. Eh, Ichiro. You open the store, maybe I get job to work for you sometimes?''

Stanley filed the pidgin phrases in his mind. Pidgin English, he figured, would surely drive his Chicago English teacher wild. One thing he noticed. In pidgin, singular and plural usually worked in reverse, and there was no such custom as number agreement of subject and verb. He noticed his father didn't answer about giving Mateo Palabang a job.

"Mateo! Sure! I knew I remembered. You change, too, you buggah!'' his father laughed.

"You been up the mainland, Ichiro?''

"Chicago. Since I'm home from the service. Long time now.''

"You no like stay in Chicago?'' There was a wistful expression on Mateo's face as if, for him, Chicago was a kind of paradise.

Stanley opened his mouth and chanced his first pidgin. "No good Chicago. More better Wainalii,'' he said tentatively.

"Eh! Too good you, Stanley!'' exclaimed his dad.

"Mo' bettah Wainalii?" repeated Mateo. "I don't think so though!"

"Mo' bettah Wainalii," Stanley insisted, pleased with himself as he watched Isaac Kaimana's sail dip over the horizon and out of sight. Strange here, yes, he thought. Different. But he was beginning to like Wainalii.

CHAPTER FOUR

In Chicago, Stanley had never had family as he did
here. Uncles. Aunts. Cousins. They all lived on the
Hilo side. The first weekend, twenty-six of them
came to Wainalii to help.

They camped in the county park. The men
rigged a tarpaulin windbreak. There were what
seemed to Stanley acres of grass mats, lauhala rugs,
and old blankets spread out on the sand. There were
lanterns to see by after dark, charcoal-burning hi-
bachis to cook the rice, big portable coolers full of ice,
beer, and soda. There were bamboo fishing poles,
shrimp nets, bait buckets, spears. Everyone worked
hard, but in between there was plenty of time to
swim, to eat, to nap, to play game after game of

sakura, with small stiff colorful Japanese cards, and listen to music on the transistor radios.

The house was the first big job. Stanley and his dad had brought one load of lumber in their truck. They had the cleaning out almost finished before the weekend. Uncle Arthur, who was Stanley's great-uncle, and the head of the big family, brought a load of roofing tins, pipes, and more lumber in his truck on Saturday morning. Kenneth brought Stanley's mother, his two sisters, and his grandmother.

All, except Uncle Arthur and Aunt Hatsu, arrived on Friday night. "You know Aunt Hatsu!" said Kenneth. "She always has to do things her way." Before he ever dreamed he would come to live in the islands and get to know her, Stanley had heard about Aunt Hatsu, who was a picture bride. Widowed and lonely, Uncle Arthur had followed old-fashioned custom a few years ago and chosen a new wife from a number of photographs sent to him by a matchmaker in Japan. "Better he chose from a tape recording!" Gobo said. Aunt Hatsu was stout and noisy. Three long black hairs grew from a mole on her chin. Uncle Arthur walked beside her looking apologetic.

Saturday morning he and Aunt Hatsu stopped at the park first to unload their bedding and food. Stanley got into the truck cab to ride along with them to the store. Aunt Hatsu was dressed to work. A bleached rice sack was tied for a scarf over her hair.

An apron protected her dress. She wore rubber zoris on her feet.

"Stop. Stop! Eh, you!" she scolded Uncle Arthur as he turned to drive up the steep incline to the courtyard. She opened the door of the truck. "Better you get out too," she ordered Stanley. "I don't trust his driving up a steep place."

Stanley, abashed, looked from her to Uncle Arthur, who was a thin, bowlegged old man with a meek face. "No pilikia. Maybe she's right," said Uncle Arthur. "Better do as she says."

Reluctantly, Stanley got down from the truck cab. He followed Aunt Hatsu up the driveway. Her face was bathed in sweat. She panted so that Stanley watched her with alarm. "I'm all right. Go. Help your mother," she said in a cross way when Stanley stopped to see if anything was wrong. His mother was carrying rubbish from the shed where the toilet, shower, *furo*, and washtubs were located. To go outside the house for these, was going to be different from Chicago. He wondered what his mother was thinking with such a strange expression on her face.

Gobo, the plumber cousin, was inside the shed tearing out the old rusted pipes. Cousin Kenneth was on the house roof with Stanley's father, repairing roofing tins. Sheryl and Louise, Stanley's small sisters, were playing with a big gang of small cousins.

Stanley noticed how everyone, even the little second cousins, paused to hear Aunt Hatsu's impressions of Wainalii.

"Mmmm." Aunt Hatsu wiped the sweat from her face with her apron. She walked over and tapped one of the posts supporting the store porch. "I thought so!" She gestured to a drift of coarse brown droppings. "Termites! The place is ready to fall down."

She stepped back and frowned at the roof. She frowned at the broken, boarded windows. She picked up a stick and poked at a wasp nest under the eaves.

"I hope she gets stung!" Stanley whispered to his mother.

"Shhhhh! Stanley!"

With intermittent unfavorable comments, Aunt Hatsu went up to the house and through each of the small rooms. She climbed down the verandah steps like a battleship negotiating a sea-lane full of mines. She looked with a grunt of disapproval into the bathhouse where Gobo resumed banging away at the pipes.

"Arthur!" she commanded. "Ichiro's your nephew. You tell him!" Then, before Uncle Arthur could imagine what it was she wanted him to say, she turned to Stanley's father. "Better you come down here and listen!"

40

Stanley watched his father hesitate, look down at his mother, then lay down his hammer and climb down from the roof.

"I thought so!" said Aunt Hatsu before his feet were off the lowest rung of the ladder. "I knew this is how it would look! The way you treat your women, you men are fifty years behind the times! Still acting like your wife was a piece of furniture with no more of a mind of her own than a noodle strainer. Ahhhhh!" Her chins, the mole, the hairs on the mole, quivered with emotion. "You never bring her to see this place until you already made up your mind. Until you're here and nothing she can do or say!" She made a single contemptuous gesture that included store, house, outbuildings, six acres, and all Wainalii. "This place is impossible!" she pronounced.

Stanley wished he hadn't eaten breakfast. It felt like everything he'd eaten was on its way back up.

"Now! Hatsu!" Uncle Arthur chided in his mild, embarrassed way.

Maizie, Kenneth's wife, and Helen, Gobo's fat jolly wife, quickly shooed all the younger children into the mango grove to play. The cousins unloading the truck began making an extra noisy clatter of stacking the lumber and pieces of roofing tin. Kenneth banged and clanked his prybar against a section of the roof.

41

"It's not what you see with your eyes looking at this place. It's the potential!" Stanley listened with apprehension to the pleading sound of his father's voice. "Six acres fee simple! The site . . . The view . . ."

"You can't eat a view," said Aunt Hatsu.

"Hatsu. Please!" begged Uncle Arthur.

She ignored him. "Sueko, better you speak your mind about this place now before you get so far into it you can't leave."

There was a troubled pause. Stanley waited, worrying, for his mother's reply. It seemed to him she was trying to make up her mind. She looked at his father, then up at the house, then up to where Sheryl and Louise were playing in the mango grove. She looked at him. Stanley felt uneasy looking back at her.

"If this is what Ichiro wants, I think it will work out," she said quietly, after what struck Stanley as much too long a time.

"You hear, Hatsu?" his dad exclaimed.

Stanley tried in vain to read either enthusiasm or certainty in his mother's expression. His dad seemed to assume both.

"I told you she feels like I do about this!"

"Mmmm," said Aunt Hatsu, doubtfully. She grabbed a rake from the truck bed and bustled to the

42

far side of the courtyard. "It would never suit me!" she complained.

All day, Stanley's father and Kenneth worked repairing the house roof. Uncle Arthur and some of the others worked at carpentering. Gobo fixed the bathhouse. Ba-chan, Aunt Hatsu, his mother, Maizie, and Helen raked, scrubbed the bathhouse walls and concrete floor and tub and took turns keeping the young children happy. When the little ones tired of running back and forth under the mango trees, hiding from each other, or playing tag, Helen—who was the kind of person that made Stanley feel good just to look at her—took all of them down to the beach to play in the sand and swim.

Bimbo and Roger, the two cousins nearest Stanley's age, went down to the beach, too, but Stanley kept on running errands for the men. He fetched tools and drinks of water and pieces of roofing tin or lumber. He held down loose ends when there was hammering to be done. He hunted the right amount of certain-sized nails for Uncle Arthur from the tool box in the bed of the truck. He helped Gobo measure and cut and fit lengths of pipe. He tended the rubbish fire when the women went down on the beach to cook the rice.

At sunset, Stanley could not remember ever having been hungrier or more tired. He took his turn in the bathhouse with the men, soaping and showering clean in the tepid water that the sun warmed. Then, like them, he sat for a long time, soaking his clean body in the deep hot water of the concrete *furo*. He put on the clean old shorts and T-shirt in which he would sleep tonight and work tomorrow. He walked to the beach in the last dim reflection of pink light from the sunset.

He flopped on a mat, his arms and legs aching, his eyelids heavy. He wondered how Bimbo and Roger could still have the energy to run up and down the hard tide-wet edge of the sand chasing crabs with their flashlights. Only his hunger and the good smell of barbecue broiling over the charcoal kept him awake. He ate two helpings of everything. He was down on his mat, half-asleep, when the men began gathering the gear and pumping gas lanterns to go night fishing.

"You coming Stanley? Or too tired?" his father asked.

Stanley managed to get up. "Sure," he said. "I'm going." You never knew. If he stayed back, he might miss something. Yawning, he pulled on a sweat shirt. The air was chilly after the intense heat of the day.

His sisters were already asleep. Only he, Bimbo,

and Roger went along with the men. Bimbo and Roger raced ahead with their flashlights stabbing at the darkness, hunting the long slanting tunnels of crabs. The crabs were fast and wary. So were the two boys. They would sneak up on a crab hole, make one lightning scoop with their hands, rush to dump the crab in Uncle Arthur's bucket, and run on ahead. Each time they caught one, they yelled. As Stanley grew less sleepy, he ran ahead with them, but he did not have their knack. He'd never tried catching crabs before. Each time he missed one, which was most of the time, Bimbo and Roger yelled with as much enthusiasm as if he'd had success. "Nevah mind. Next time you get one okay!" Bimbo would encourage on each try.

They went in the same direction Stanley had come that first morning when he had set off to do his own exploring. The lanterns and flashlights cast odd shadows over the kiawes edging the beach, the dense barricade of kiawe on the point ahead, and the starlit sheen of the water. The tide was low.

"Spooky, yuh?" said Bimbo delightedly.

"Spooky," agreed Stanley. He was uneasy, coming this way in the darkness. He wished Roger would quit acting like such a little kid and making funny noises. "Ghosts! *Obaki!*" squealed Roger.

"Ahhhhh," scoffed Stanley. If Roger and Bimbo

only knew, he thought, they would not be making a joke of what was, over here, something very real. This close, and his heart was already pounding with fear. He dropped behind, out of the crab hunting, back with the men.

They waded around the point. The flashlights probing ahead pointed out the exposed tidal lava and the tiny sand crescent of beach. In the water, small bright red fish stayed mesmerized for an instant in the light. The gas lanterns held high illuminated a considerable expanse of the surface. "Look!" urged Kenneth.

An eel, thick as Stanley's wrist and long as a good-sized snake, writhed across the border of light and darkness. "Eh, the kind *puhi*! I scare!" yelled Bimbo. They all hurried up onto the sand. Kenneth took his spear and waded out, lantern held high, spear poised to jab.

Stanley could not control his shivers.

"Me, I don't like those *puhi*, those big eels either," said his father.

"When they bite, they rake the flesh down to your bones," said Gobo. "I know. One time I was fishing with a man. He was cleaning fish by a rock. He put his hand in the water to rinse off the fish. This *puhi* was there waiting. They like to eat the guts of the fish, the fish, anything they can get. I tell you. I figure nothing could make a bite like that eel.

46

Forty-one stitches to sew that man's hand back in one piece at the hospital!"

"Wow," said Stanley. At the moment he was far less apprehensive about any eel than about being this close to the hidden clearing.

"Cold?" asked his father.

"A little," Stanley lied. He hugged his arms to his chest, keeping as close to the water's edge as he dared. The light from behind walked with him, wavering and bobbing over into the wall of thorny branches. Stanley could not keep from looking. There it was in the swaying halo from the gas lantern. The place where he had ducked in under the low-hanging branches.

He stopped, abruptly. "Hey!" A branch was broken and pushed aside. A line of footprints, fresh ones, tracked across the sand and onto the faint trail.

"Big feet, that buggah!" marveled Gobo. He aimed a flashlight at the footprints. Bare feet, long, wide, with the splayed toes of someone who was used to walking without shoes.

Stanley turned and ran. He stopped in water up to his ankles, beside Kenneth.

"Whatsa mattah you?" asked Gobo.

"Ah. He got away!" said Kenneth, retrieving his spear.

"Who?" shuddered Stanley, his mind only on the footprints leading into the clearing, and the size of them, and who might have gone in there, and why.

Kenneth turned to him with an astonished laugh. "Who?" he repeated. "Who do you think? The eel, of course!"

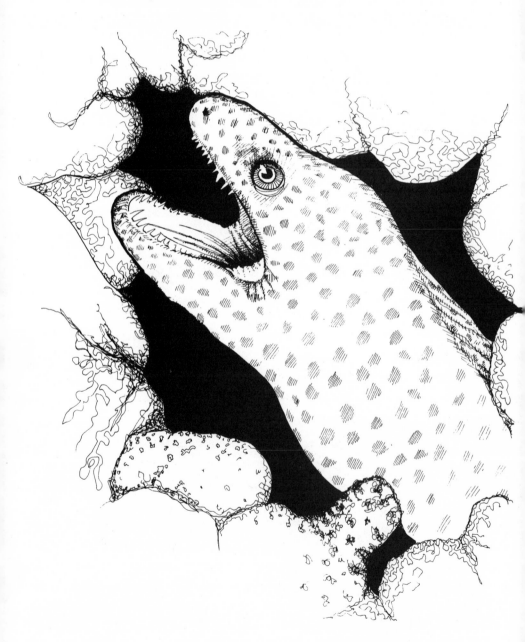

CHAPTER FIVE

Stanley had not imagined how it might be to live
without electricity. Switches, bulbs, water heaters,
refrigerators, fans, TV's, radios, toasters, vacuum
cleaners, his father's electric razor, his mother's sew-
ing machine: these he had taken for granted. They
had been a necessary part of life, as expectable as air
to breathe and water coming out of a faucet for
drinking, cooking, bathing, and doing the laundry.

At Wainalii, the water source for the faucets was
not that dependable either. The water tank for each
household, including his own, had to be filled by rain
or by water hauled in trucks down the mountainside.

The only modern convenience was the telephone. One line, for sixteen families, came down the

mountainside from the ranch town twelve rough miles away.

At night the yellow glow of kerosene lamps and the hard blue-white glare of gas lanterns shone out through the open windows and doors of the houses. In the kitchen of their house was a gas stove fed from a propane tank outside. There was the same kind of refrigerator. There was not a light switch or fixture or base plug in house or store or bathhouse or storage sheds. Only hooks on which to suspend lanterns.

"One day when we get a little money ahead, we'll put a generator back by the mango grove," Stanley's dad planned. He was so full of enthusiasm and ideas that he never noticed what kept bothering Stanley. "Eh, Sueko! Our gold mine! Our lucky break, yuh?" he exclaimed when the day came that they could move into the house. There was no answer, no comment at all.

Stanley, watching the unfamiliar bleak expression on his mother's face, began to wonder. Without complaint, his mother worked as hard as the rest of them, but she was too quiet and too strained and unlike herself. She wasn't going to be happy here, Stanley could tell.

Every morning at eight o'clock Stanley was there when the opening bell rang in the Wainalii school. It was a big, airy building set up off the ground on stilts like the village houses, with a broad verandah and a long flight of wooden steps. The play yard was bare earth. There were hibiscus hedges around the school building and screening each of the outhouses.

The nine grades sat in one room with one teacher. There were nineteen pupils. Stanley was the lone ninth grader. Every morning Mrs. Kainoa, the teacher, assigned him lessons to do by himself in English, math, science, and social studies. If he did not understand something, he could ask her for help. Every afternoon, or earlier if he finished, she checked his work. Music, art, and the basketball or baseball that Mrs. Kainoa called P.E. were done by all nine grades together. Once in a while a visiting teacher came to talk about science or tell them stories. There were library books in one corner and two sets of encyclopedias with colored pictures. When his work was done, Stanley was free to leave his desk and read anything he chose, or draw, or just sit and daydream.

It was not the same as school in Chicago had been. Once he got used to it, Stanley could not imagine how he could have survived his old buzzer-signaled period-changing school day of a different subject every forty minutes with a different teacher in a different room. This way, when he finished the assignments in his books, he could read or look up anything he chose. He could take all day, or two hours, to do the lessons, and do them in any order that appealed to him. Some days he fooled around until two o'clock before starting his work. Some days he hurried, and then spent hours leafing through volumes of the encyclopedia, stopping to find out about any subject that caught his interest. He began to like just sitting and reading books that nobody said he had to read. Sometimes he spent two hours drawing elaborate pictures of racing cars, or airplanes, or submarines he was going to invent maybe someday. Sometimes Mrs. Kainoa asked him to help one of the younger grades with arithmetic, which he liked.

His mother kept after him every day. "No homework?"

"No homework."

"Did you learn anything today?"

"Oh—" Stanley was never quite sure. How could he tell what it really was his mother wanted him to say. The simplest answer, but not the right one, was, "I don't know," to which he always added quickly, "Lots of things."

"You did your work in school?"

"Sure."

"You were a good boy?"

"I guess so."

"The teacher heard your lessons?"

Stanley soon knew every question in his mother's afternoon catechism about school. He also understood, from the way she and his dad began arguing about it, that Wainalii school was another of the misgivings his mother had about living here.

"No worry. He's a bright boy. He'll do all right. He's young yet," his dad kept insisting. Next year, for high school, Stanley would ride the school bus thirty-four miles up the mountainside at half-past six every morning. Kenneth, the teacher, had assured them it was a good high school. The trouble was, he tended to agree with Stanley's mother about how much anyone got from the one-room school. "I don't know," Kenneth kept commenting, "Mrs. Kainoa, she doesn't have her degree—only a normal school certificate."

Stanley could not see what difference that made. All that mattered to him was that school no longer was a boring, time-eating part of his life. And there was so much to do and see and learn and listen to during the other hours of the day.

Whenever he could, if he were ready for school and saw Isaac Kaimana out early to launch his canoe, Stanley would go down to the beach to watch. As many times as he did, he could not make himself believe what his eyes were seeing. The black canoe setting out with the barracuda following it. It was too odd to be credible and yet there it was—just as there was the stone shark hidden in its clearing.

Stanley soon knew all the other eighteen kids in school. Three of them were Kaimanas: Junior, in seventh grade, Kimo in fifth, Iwalani in second. Junior and Kimo were built like their father. Iwalani was small and slight. Once in a while Lester Ching or the Ii twins or Darwin Pahanui would tease Iwalani about how different she was from the rest of the family until Junior would threaten to bust them up. Junior Kaimana and Darwin Pahanui and Stanley were the oldest in the school. The three of them soon became good friends, but even so Stanley did not contemplate asking Junior or Kimo about the barracuda that fished with their father, or about the footprints that had led into the shark-stone clearing, or about the stone. Nobody had to tell him. He knew by intuition. These were questions you didn't ask in Wainalii.

Wainalii was the friendliest place Stanley had ever been. The only person in the village who had not been up offering to help or getting acquainted was Isaac Kaimana. Stanley guessed, from the way others talked about him, that Junior's father kept aloof from everyone—he was respected, but left alone, as he seemed to prefer.

Many from the village remembered Ichiro from when he was a boy. They were as confused as Mateo Palabang had been about why anyone from the mainland would want to settle in this small isolated place, but they were pleased. Since last year, with the old store closed, they had had to drive the long bumpy miles up the mountain whether they needed a big grocery order or some emergency so small as a loaf of bread, a pack of cigarettes, or a six-pack of beer.

Opening day, Stanley was out at six helping his father unlock the doors. The first customer was already on his way up the steep drive. It was Isaac Kaimana. Stanley's mother started down from the house, took one look at him, and turned around. She did not like the habit Wainalii men had of going without a shirt, which was how Isaac had dressed this morning.

Isaac glanced at Stanley and nodded a greeting as if he remembered him from the beach. He walked across the courtyard and into the store. Stanley and his dad followed.

Isaac turned and handed an empty gallon jug to Stanley. "Get kerosene?"

Quickly, Stanley searched his new memory bank of pidgin.

"Get," he answered. He went to the hundred-gallon drum at the side of the building and filled Isaac's jug. He turned the spigot on and off with great care, not spilling one drop. He screwed the cap tight. He wiped the jug with a rag. Then he walked back into the store and handed the jug to their first customer. Their first sale. He shared a silent jubilation with his dad.

Isaac took a dollar bill from the pocket of his shorts.

"Cash?" Stanley noted how pleased his father

was. One of the worries of storekeeping that Uncle Arthur had advised them to accept before they came over here was that most in Wainalii would want to trade on credit. Hawaiians, Uncle Arthur confided without letting Aunt Hatsu hear him, could be a poor risk, and there might be relatives of Uncle Kenji's wife who still felt a family obligation was due.

"Cash today," Isaac shrugged. The flash of a smile crossed his face. This glimpse of humor, as if Isaac had known what had been going through Stanley's mind and been amused by it, made Stanley feel more at ease.

"Take a look around!" Mr. Sasaki urged, handing Isaac his change. Isaac hesitated. He gave Stanley and his dad a peculiar searching glance. "Okay," he said, as if one of them must know what was bothering him, "I take one look around."

Stanley backed out of his way and stood leaning against the door frame. Slowly, studying every label and price mark, Isaac surveyed the stock on the newly refinished shelves. Canned goods, paper picnic supplies, a few bolts of yard goods, and assorted sizes of T-shirts and shorts. The refrigerator counter stocked with oranges and apples, packaged lunch meats and cheese, chocolate bars, and eggs. Sacks of poi, the purplish starchy paste that the people in Wainalii ate as much of and as often as Stanley's family ate rice or others might eat potatoes and bread. Boxes of sugar.

Boxes of powdered milk. Fifty-pound sacks of rice, since some Wainalii people ate both rice and poi. Glass jars full of cellophane-wrapped packages of Chinese noodles, whole dried codfish, dried abalone, dried squid.

A wire display rack held bags of potato chips, Chinese seeds flavored with salt, sugar, licorice, and eaten like candy. A rack for comic books, paperbacks with lurid covers, and magazines. A glassed case on the counter for small popular items that might otherwise walk out of the store in a pocket: chewing gum, Sen-Sen, the cough drops that Stanley had learned were used as candy over here.

On overhead racks, and wall racks, and in other glass display cases were bamboo poles, nylon fishline, hooks and sinkers of every size, lures for spinning and casting rods, shrimp nets, papier-mâché bait buckets, inflatable plastic beach toys, flashlight batteries, suntan lotion, camera film, swim fins, masks, snorkels. A double-doored refrigerator was filled with milk and soft drinks and another with beer.

Isaac Kaimana took his time looking. "Eh," he said when he finished. "You really stock up. All kinds." He reached into one refrigerator, helped himself to a bottle of coke, pried off the cap with his teeth, and put more money on the counter. He drank the coke in one long effervescent swig. "Ahhhhh," he put the empty bottle in the case on the floor. Then, leaning against the refrigerator doors he folded his arms across his enormous bare chest. "You Hilo boy, Sasaki?"

"That's right."

"You stay up the mainland until now?"

"Chicago."

"Your uncle, he left this place to you?"

"Yes."

Isaac nodded. He looked at Stanley. He looked at Mr. Sasaki. To Stanley, Isaac's eyes seemed to be able to prove the privacy of one's mind.

"I wonder to myself when I hear about you folks coming," said Isaac. "Why? Everybody else these days leaving this island, moving to Honolulu or to the mainland to stay. Like you did yourself years ago."

Stanley's father smiled. "I'm the one reversing the trend. Wainalii–this is the dream I carried around all this time in my head! The weather? Who can beat it. The atmosphere. The scenery. The people. The potential!" He leaned forward, thumping the counter with his fist for emphasis. "When I was young like Stanley, I already made up my mind, if the chance came, all what I want for the rest of my life is to wake up every morning and be able to look down out of this courtyard and see the ocean and the seabeach and the houses and the palm grove and the view. So–lucky for me! I have the chance, thanks to my uncle's remembering me in his will. And my family wanted to come too."

Isaac gave them each a peculiar glance. "I like what you say, Sasaki. Only, more to this place than you look out with your eyes and see from this courtyard every morning. No?" He picked up the kerosene jug. "See you," he said. With a proud, elegant stride, he walked out of the store.

Stanley followed his father to the doorway and watched Isaac Kaimana disappear down the drive, across the road, and into the palm grove.

"More to this place than you can see with your eyes. What did he mean by that?"

Stanley didn't answer. He knew. He knew that Isaac Kaimana knew he knew. Standing here, with this queer scared feeling, Stanley figured there must be something he ought to do about it, but he didn't know what.

CHAPTER SIX

The store was open seven days a week, from six-thirty in the morning until ten o'clock at night. They were all up early. While his dad enjoyed a cup of coffee out at the edge of the courtyard, Stanley used the first free time of his day to run down and explore the beach in the dawn, to watch Isaac Kaimana on the mornings he left with his *kaku,* to watch other fishermen returning in their canoes from a night of bottom fishing.

By half-past six, he was back home, had eaten breakfast, and was into the day's chores. He swept out the store, then ran a feather duster over what stock he could before he left for school. After school, he was usually home before his dad returned from his twice-weekly trips up the mountainside for supplies and the mail. A quick snack, then Stanley began work again. More dusting. Replenishing the refrigerator with soda. Pricing and restocking the canned goods on the shelves. Late in the afternoon when his mother had finished her own work, she came down to tend store for an hour while he and his dad went off—sometimes for a swim, sometimes for an hour of fishing, sometimes just to sit on the beach and talk or to take the two little girls to hunt shells.

It was nearing dusk one afternoon when the two of them started out. Stanley didn't mind having his sisters along, but they spent a long part of their days on the beach with Ba-chan. He liked best these afternoons he and his dad had to themselves. Today they walked to the village beach where Isaac Kaimana and his wife Queenie, and Junior, Kimo, and Iwalani sat cleaning and salting a washtub of opelu.

"*Holoholo?*" Junior asked Stanley.

"I guess. Too late for swim. No good tide for fish." Stanley spoke pidgin with such determination that Junior had to laugh at him. "Eh, you Stanley," Junior admired, "you no talk like one haole anymore."

Pleased, Stanley went over to the edge of the water and skipped a few stones to try his skill. He listened to his father and Isaac talking about the ocean. There was rough weather somewhere out at sea. Big swells were booming up on the reef at the entrance

61

to the bay. When it was calm, skipping flat water-smoothed pieces of coral or lava was easy. Tonight, not so. After a while, the two men stopped talking.

Mr. Sasaki strolled on up the beach, Stanley lagging behind hunting for shells and making a lunge at stray crabs. Only when they came to the rocky point at the detour on the trail did Stanley realize where they were heading.

His dad splashed on around the point. Reluctantly Stanley followed.

"Like before!" exclaimed his father at the sight of big bare footprints across the wet sand. They led to the edge of the kiawes and the entrance of the faint trail.

Stanley started to warn his father not to follow where those tracks led. Then, on second thought, he closed his mouth. Had the shark stone really been all he imagined it? Maybe, if he forced himself to go back and look when he was not alone— It took all his willpower, all his courage to walk in the line of those footprints, as his father was.

His father stooped and went along under the broken branch, up the trace of trail. Stanley stooped, and shuddered, and kept close behind. The footprints were visible on the soft ground under the kiawes and the trail itself less obstructed than Stanley had remembered. It was gloomy in the red light.

62

Stanley jumped at the groaning creak of one kiawe branch rubbing against another. "Spooky place this time of night!" said his father cheerily.

"I'll say," Stanley agreed. As they groped along, the thought occurred to him. Perhaps in some mysterious way the shark stone was gone, and there would be nothing to see, nothing to give him that awful feeling.

"Ah!"

His father stopped so fast that Stanley stumbled against him. He grabbed his father's shirt and peered around him into the clearing. It made no difference at all not to be alone. It had not gone away. It had not been his imagination. There it was, exactly as before: the long black shark-shaped stone, the stone eyes that seemed to look back at them, the eerie sense the stone gave of being alive.

Stanley's heart pounded as though it would burst. He felt sweaty and chilled both at the same time. He wanted to say "Let's go!" but his voice was lost in a choked scared feeling in his throat. He tried to pull back. Instead, his father went on into the clearing, closer to the stone.

"I'm going!" Stanley whispered. He turned and ran out, careless of the thorny branches, his feet racing faster and faster until he was safe in the open sunset sky on the beach. He stood and waited and hugged his arms across his chest to try to keep from shaking. It was five minutes that seemed like fifty before his father came out.

"You been in there before? You knew that was there?"

Stanley nodded.

"I never saw one before." Mr. Sasaki put a hand on Stanley's shoulder and stood, staring at the ocean, saying nothing, for a long time. One what, Stanley wanted to ask.

When they started back, he kept close to his dad, wondering now if it were dark enough to worry about *puhi*. They hurried back to Wainalii beach, past the deserted park, along the stone wall, avoiding going into or through the village. On the road they met Mateo Palabang walking along stroking a rooster that was cradled in the crook of his arm. It was no ordinary rooster, Stanley knew. That one was Mateo's favorite fighting cock.

"Hey, Ichiro! You like come see one chicken fight?" Mateo invited.

"Not tonight. Thanks, Mateo. Next time, okay?"

When Mateo was out of hearing, before they reached the driveway to the store, Stanley asked, "You said you never saw one before. One what? You know what it is? That's something bad, that stone in there?"

His dad looked toward the lanterns where the Kaimanas sat on the beach cleaning fish. "I don't know," he said in a way that troubled Stanley. "I heard, but I never believed before." They turned up the drive. "You never said anything to anybody about seeing it? To Junior? Or Kimo? Or your mother?"

Stanley shook his head.

"Don't," said his father in a low voice, "don't say anything about where we went to anyone!"

CHAPTER SEVEN

Stanley had had his bath and was sitting listening to his transistor radio on the store steps when Isaac Kaimana came up the driveway with a flashlight in one hand and a bucket of fish in the other. All Stanley could think of, watching those big bare feet coming toward him, were the footprints leading into the kiawe and the clearing below.

Isaac Kaimana switched off his flashlight as Mr. Sasaki came out with his lantern to lock up the store.

"Ah, Isaac!" Stanley could hear the uneasiness in his dad's voice.

"You folks like papio?" Isaac asked, handing Stanley the bucket of fish.

Mr. Sasaki's wary expression altered. "Thank

you!" He admired the blue bodies of the fish staring up at him with their big gelatinous eyes. Stanley shut off his radio and started up to the house with the bucket.

"Stanley!" Isaac called to him. "You come back, after you give your momma the fish!"

When he came back, the two men were sitting on the store steps beside the lantern in a silence that felt noisy.

"Stanley. Bring us one soda," said his dad.

Stanley brought out three bottles of orange. As before, Isaac opened his with his teeth. "Wow!" Stanley marveled. He tried, but it hurt.

"No! Maybe you break 'em if you don't have the knack!" Isaac cautioned.

"Don't try it! No dentist around here, you know." His dad passed him the opener.

It seemed an uncomfortably long time to Stanley that they sat drinking soda and saying nothing. Finally Isaac cleared his throat. "Okay. We talk. You know what I mean about, Sasaki? You, you're island born. I think you know where you supposed to go and where you supposed not to go looking around when you walk up the beach, yuh?" His stare was an accusation.

"If you mean we weren't supposed to go inside the clearing and see the shark stone? Eh! No sign kapu. No fence. No walls. Nobody tells us. How we know you don't want us in there?" Stanley was surprised by the anger with which his father spoke.

"No need you get *huhu!*" Isaac raised his hand. "Strange people they went in there before and saw him. They don't say nothing. They don't do nothing. They don't even know who he is. Only you. You knew, yuh Sasaki? You and your boy?"

"Who *he* is?" Stanley repeated. A shiver ran the length of his spine. A draft seemed to rise from nowhere out of the balmy still night air. He rubbed at the gooseflesh that prickled his forearms and moved closer to his dad.

"He. The stone. The big black stone who is a shark," said Isaac. "What surprise me," he went on as matter of factly as if he were discussing some trouble with his outboard engine, "is that he show himself like that to you. So I had to tell him all about you, Stanley, and how come you are around, one stranger, walking into his kapu place. Okay. He understand now. I tell him about you. Then tonight, the both of you went inside there, so I think no use wait to talk to you. You better know, how come he stays inside there, how come that beach is kapu."

Stanley kept rubbing his arms, feeling as he did sometimes in the night when he woke up in the grip of a powerful nightmare.

Isaac reached behind and put out the lantern.

68

"No good keep this on. If it's dark up here, nobody will come bother us."

Slowly, the darkness became less black. The band of the Milky Way, the multitude of stars in the clear sky, the rising moon, restored the buildings and trees and the road below to more familiar reassuring shapes and shadows.

"Stanley?" his mother called from the house.

"He's talking with us. Isaac Kaimana is here," his dad called back.

"Okay," Isaac repeated. "This is a good time, tonight. I tell you the story. This happened maybe two hundred, maybe three hundred years ago." Isaac's eyes were fixed on the far starlit horizon of sea and sky and Maui. He seemed to have dropped into a trance, oblivious of the courtyard, the store, even— Stanley guessed—himself and his father.

"Two? Three hundred years? About like that. My grandmother, who gave this story on to me, and gave the care of him over to me, the way she told, this all happen before my grandmother's grandmother's grandmother was a young girl. Wainalii? The same, then. This is an ancient place. Only all grass houses built on stone platforms those days. This was a big important village then. Plenty houses. Plenty people. Plenty the kind mana—" Isaac paused. "Mana," he repeated. "Stanley, I like for you to understand that Hawaiian word. Mana. A special kind of power. Spirit power. The power you have inside yourself and that rocks can have, and all creatures. Like kaku. Like sharks." He paused again. "You understand?"

Stanley nodded. Mana, he whispered to himself. That must be what he sensed in the hidden big black stone that looked and listened and seemed alive.

"Strong then. Still can be strong now—for some of us," Isaac continued. "So it was one time then long, long ago when my grandmother's grandmother's grandmother went all by herself one day to the kapu beach to look for opihi and swim. She was good looking, this girl. Always the men and boys, they chase after her. Only, this day, no boyfriend, no man friend, no girl friend. She want to be off by herself all alone.

"That place (you know where I mean, Stanley!) People didn't go there then like the people in Wainalii don't hang around that kapu beach now. They pass by way out in the water when they go that direction for fishing. The kids now, they call that place 'ghost beach.'" Isaac gave a funny smile. "They don't know nothing, they don't want to know nothing, my own kids, about what it is when a place is kapu, or for why. All they know is—don't hang around there." He nodded at Stanley's stifled exclamation. "That's right. That's why you never see anybody down there. Even my Iwalani, my little one, she could tell you—don't go that place. Only they don't know why. And they don't know you been there. Only me. I knew."

Isaac's voice resumed a chanting rhythm. "This young girl, my grandmother's grandmother's grandmother, she's the independent kind. Saucy. She goes where she wants. She is alii, chief's family, but not so highborn that they watch too close over her.

"This certain day she felt the urge. She like to go to the kapu beach to look for opihi and swim. All her family, all her friends, the high chiefs, the kahunas, the guards, everybody but herself and one old man she don't know about, they went up into the mountains that day. She wait. She hide. Everybody gone, she thinks, so she runs down to the kapu beach. She looks for opihi. Kapu, too, those opihi, but she picks them and eats them. Nothing happen. This made her feel brave, more saucy, so all by herself she went for a swim. Those days kapu didn't mean keep out, like now Stanley. Those days, you go to a kapu place or do a kapu thing, or eat one kapu food and the kahuna finds out—you die!

"Eh, that wahine! She swam out over the coral heads into deep water. She dived and played. She had a good time by herself until the old man who she didn't know was left behind, an old man who kept to himself away from the rest of the village people, came along the beach and shouted, 'Get out of the water, girl! I warn you! Hurry for your life!'

"Why did this old man shout so at her, she wonders. She looked all around to see what was it, so dangerous he tell to her. Then, she laughs. She had not noticed before, but now she saw a young man swimming near her. His smile flashed like the white crest of waves breaking. His eyes flirted. He raised a strong arm and motioned for her to come swimming farther out with him.

" 'No, no! Swim ashore for your life!' the old man called. Then, he shouted something in a language the girl did not understand.

"Ah, she thought, what is the matter with him? I like young men. She looked over her shoulder, to flirt a little with the handsome stranger. But his smile, his good-looking face, his beckoning arm, were gone.

"Instead, the black fin of a shark cut in a circle close to her in the blue water. Auwe! How she swam then! Her heart pounded with fear. Her long hair was a black cloud like squid ink all over the surface of the water.

"When she got into shallow water where the coral grew close to the surface, she stood up. She looked back. There swam the young man calling to her from the deep blue water.

"Scared now, though, this young girl. She hurry out on the sand. She look from the beach one more time at the ocean. The young man had changed himself into a shark!

" 'Auwe!' she began to cry. 'What is that? Who is that? What happens out there?'

" 'A good-looking girl like you should never swim this place!' the old man scolded her. 'Now you see why kapu? When he's a young man, he gets ideas like any young man, but he is so restless that right away, when he gets excited, he changes himself into a shark and a shark has a different appetite. It's my fault. I am getting too old to take care anymore. Often, I cannot come when he needs me.'

" 'He? Who do you mean, he?' said my grandmother's grandmother's grandmother, this young girl. (Like you asked me tonight, Stanley," Isaac reminded.)

"For answer, the old man tell to her, 'Come. I show you. I make you understand.' He lead her back along the beach, where there was no kiawe growing those days, but a milo thicket (and still a milo thicket, and hala trees—pandanus, guarding that clearing when my own grandmother was taken first time for see the stone.)

" 'No, no! Kapu!' The young girl didn't want to go.

" 'Kapu I make only for his sake, to protect him

73

and to protect people like yourself,' said the old man. 'No scare. Come!'

"So, she follow him, to the same clearing where he likes to stay still yet today, that big black stone. 'This is where he lives. Here is the young man who called you, the big black shark who chased you,' said the old man. 'Lucky for you, girl, I came along this beach when I did. He would have had the shark's way, not the young man's way with you!'

" 'I tell you who he is. This one was *naha*, highest born chief, a young prince. My father sent me to be in his court when I was a boy. This young chief, his god was the shark god and whenever the sharks come into the bay, certain seasons, the rest of us hurry out on the beach, but not this one! No, no. Never he! He play with those sharks. He speak to them in their own language. To him, the shark was companion—no different from human companion except, as we grew up, he and I together, he liked the shark's company more.

" 'One day his father, the king, said to him. 'How is this? Are you my son a human, or are you my son, a shark? Answer this for me!'

" 'Whichever I choose to be, I am. I have that power. I have strong mana,' said the young man, proud, and from that day he would change himself from one to the other, whichever form—human or shark—he wanted to be.

74

" 'People became afraid of him. He kept to this bay, and this beach, and no one came near except for me.

" 'One day this man-shark told me, "I am not happy in either form any longer. My power is strong enough, so now I shall change to the shape of a stone. A stone can be quiet and nobody bothering him. A stone can stay in one place and be alone, hidden. I promise you. I will use this power to protect whoever watches over me and keeps people out of my way. I will speak to the sharks, my brothers, to help me in this. Only remember, always, I am a stone, who can if I choose go back to the shape of a shark anytime and even—if I am so tempted—I can take back the form of a man!"

" 'But how is it I never hear this before, from anyone else in the village?' the young girl asks him.

" 'For a while, before you were born, this was much talked of, when I asked the shark stone's father to pronounce this place kapu. Many were scared. They did not want to talk about it, or think about it. They forget because they want to forget. They know this bay and beach, kapu—but they don't want to remember why.

" 'Now you know,' said the old man. 'And all these years, you are the only person, the only human besides myself, to whom he has shown himself. I take this as a sign. I am old. I have no family to carry on for me. Soon, I think, I am going to die. Will you take on the care of this stone, as I will teach to you, and pass the care of him on to someone in your family before you die?'"

Isaac leaned forward, his motion jolting the step on which they all sat in a way that made Stanley jump.

"This girl," said Isaac, "my ancestor, did not know what to say to the old man. 'Let me think a while,' she asked. She walked out to the place where she had left her opihis. She picked them up. She walked back slowly, slowly into the milo thicket, to the clearing and the shark stone and the old man.

"She looked into the stone eyes of the shark. She could feel his power strong, all around in the clearing. 'Auwe!' she said, 'If I do not do this favor, all my life I will not feel easy to go again past this place or out anywhere into the sea. So, this thing has happened. You have asked,' she told the old man, 'and my answer to you is yes. I will take care of him for you.' As she spoke, she felt strength enter her body. Her eyes could look without fear into the eyes of the stone shark looking back at her. Her legs felt a strong pull to run and swim as long as she wished, all day and all night if she wanted, wherever in the ocean she wanted, far out into the deep blue waters of the sea.

76

" 'Then for all time to come,' said the old man, 'the shark is your aumakua. He and you are of one blood.' "

Isaac sat rigid. His hands gripped the edge of the step. "As if lightning was all around her, as if the power of mana flowed like a storm tide up over that clearing, so my grandmother's grandmother's grandmother felt there with him that first day. The old man taught her, and after he died, every day she looked after the stone. By and by she married. She gave birth to a daughter, and when that daughter was a young woman, she passed the charge of the shark stone on to her.

"Six generations, so it went, until my mother would not listen to the story her mother tried to tell her." Isaac shook his head. "She believed anything Hawaiian, old Hawaiian, was not good. She had been away to the missionary school too young." Isaac gave Stanley a swift, appraising glance. "Especially after my brother, her first born, what happened then—she was too scared. Hawaiian style, when I was born, my grandmother took me to raise. When I was six years old, she showed me the stone, she told me his story. No secret. Only people don't like to talk about such things. Now same as long time ago. They don't like to think about such things could be.

"Plenty strangers, camped down the park, they

77

went in and saw him but no matter. They think, only one big boulder. They don't recognize who he is, like you did, Stanley. First time you knew he was something, no ordinary stone. I take my time to study you. I like you, Stanley. I like what you said about why you came back to Wainalii, Ichiro. You two and me, we are going to be good friends. Nobody else have the feeling for this place, like us. Ah!'' Isaac sighed. ''That's what bother me all the time, what I think about every day, every night.

''The islands, they coming different. Honolulu—Kona—Hilo—everyplace but here, they forget how to live. They cut down the old trees. They block off the beaches with big hotels. They hide the mountain from your eyes with tall buildings. They fill up the valleys with houses what look like the mainland. The new people, they come in and pretty soon they change the place all around. And tourists. Every place get tourists. Not much left with the old island feeling, the true spirit, like Wainalii. That's why I am happy you the ones take over the store here. Not somebody going to change everything, make fancy, make hotel, spoil the place to make money.''

Stanley looked anxiously in the darkness at his father, who said nothing.

''You two,'' said Isaac with confidence, ''you the kind different. You understand. Like, you recognize the shark stone, and you feel his mana." He turned and fixed his piercing gaze on Stanley. "You understand about mana now. You know the power of his." Isaac's voice was proud. "And mine!"

CHAPTER EIGHT

When he got up next morning, Stanley had no urge
to go down to the beach. He stayed in the courtyard,
looking at the village in the pewter light before sunrise. Thatched roofs and grass houses built on stone
platforms would have seemed more natural with
Isaac's story strong in his mind.

His dad came out with his coffee and sat on the
bench under the milo tree beside him. They said
nothing. This was no time of day for talking. Especially after last night. Stanley sat there, watching and
thinking. When fishing was good, which it was now,
some of the men and a few of their women were out
all night and into the morning in their canoes. Two
canoes were coming in from the ocean now. Yama

Ching and the Alapais'. Yama Ching had been cousin to Uncle Kenji's Hawaiian wife. Emma Ching, Mrs. Alapai, and Lester Ching were standing down on the beach waiting for the canoes. None of them, Stanley reflected, lived on a regular routine the way he and his family did. One time, Lester Ching might be up and out all night. He would run from the canoe, change clothes, grab a pilot cracker, and rush to school by first bell, no sleep. Other times, he might skip school, and the whole family, if they felt like it, sleep in until noon.

Fishing, what was running and when, this was what set the inner clocks of living in Wainalii. They all worked hard, but not at the same thing day after day and not at regular hours, which was remarkable to Stanley. He had noticed how, after they got up and did a few chores and ate breakfast, some of the Wainalii people would lie down in the shade and take a nap. When he passed by on his way to school, the women who were sweeping porches or bending over their washtubs, or hanging clothes to dry on a line strung between two trees, moved with the slow, easy movements of women in a dream. Anytime of day, Stanley had seen one person or another sitting down under a tree and doing nothing. He envied the way they all lived by impulse. Fish running? Jump in the canoe and go! The water looks good for a swim? Then you swim, no matter what kind of clothes you have on. The sun is always hot. You can dry off fast. Go!

Lights still burned in some of the houses in the village this morning. Kaimanas' was one. Somebody came out on the verandah, a man, but not Isaac. Stanley looked out across the bay. Isaac's black canoe was coming in from around the lighthouse point. By the time the canoe reached the entrance through the reef, the man on Kaimanas' porch was gone. Only Queenie stood there, leaning against the railing, smoking a cigarette and idly combing her long dark hair. She was a heavy woman, big in her way as Isaac was in his, and with the same handsome bearing.

"Breakfast!"

Stanley knew, hearing his mother's call, that it was six o'clock. Below, the only other person in Wainalii who lived on a regular daily schedule, shuffled up the path from his shack, his guava walking stick poking ahead to support each step. Every morning as he went to breakfast, Stanley could depend on seeing old Ah Fook begin his walk through the palm grove. When he returned to sweep out the store after breakfast, it was half-past six and Stanley knew exactly where the ancient Chinese man would be. Sitting on the abandoned post office steps staring at a faded poster figure with a pointing finger and the bleached legend, "Uncle Sam Wants YOU."

Stanley leaned on the broom in the store entry.

He could see the black canoe pulled up on the beach under its cover of roofing tins. Queenie, Junior, Kimo, and Iwalani were on the beach cleaning fish. Isaac was on his way up the path.

"Stanley! Fetch coffee for Isaac and me," his father called as Isaac approached.

"Last night. First thing this morning. All those men think of is talk, talk, talk," his mother complained as she handed Stanley two mugs of coffee, a can of milk, the sugar bowl, and two spoons on a metal tray.

Stanley listened to her, surprised. She usually didn't say such things. "Lazy. This is a lazy place. Don't you be like them, you hear?" she admonished as Stanley maneuvered down the porch steps, balancing the two coffee cups on the tray.

The men took their coffee cups out to the bench under the milo tree. Stanley hurried over the floor with his broom and then spent a long time sweeping the store verandah and dusting the stock near the doorway, where he could watch and listen.

"You went fishing all night?" his dad was asking.

"Good time of moon," said Isaac. Below, Darwin Pahanui's father's canoe went *put-put-put* across the shadows of the bay. Mr. Pahanui and his skinny wife sat hunched as if, this hour of the morning, they were cold.

"Pahanui, he's only going for boat ride, I think.

No more fish around now." Isaac held the spoon against the side of his cup out of the way of his face while he took a cautious swallow. "No good for the stomach if too hot." He set the cup on the ground to cool.

From the house came the *whussk-whusssk* of Ba-chan's broom. Stanley could see his mother at the tubs behind the bathhouse putting the laundry to soak. Sheryl came down to the courtyard, pulling Louise in their coaster wagon. The two of them stared at Isaac Kaimana, their chubby faces solemn, sucking their fingers, eyes studying his.

"Two girls. One boy. Small family you get, Ichiro," said Isaac.

"Three. Same like you so far. October, we expecting one more."

The two men laughed together in a way that made Stanley look back at his mother. October? That, he decided, was why she was so cross lately. Complaining about all kinds of things when in Chicago he didn't remember her complaining at all.

"The three with us, they're the youngest," said Isaac. "And Queenie, she's not my first wife. Before, the times you came here for help your uncle, I was in Honolulu then. I work on the Matson freighters, back and forth, every ten days, Honolulu to San Francisco, Honolulu to L.A. Ten years like that, and I'm divorced. I marry up with Queenie. We move back here. Our first ones, all girls, Queenie gave to her mother to raise. They live Honolulu. The first, she graduate last year from business school. The second, she fool around and get married already. The others, they go Kam School. You know us Hawaiians. The first child, maybe two or three of the others. *Hanai*. Somebody wants them, so you give them away.''

Isaac drank his cooled coffee and stood up. ''I keep you from your work, Ichiro. No good.'' He stopped and put his empty cup on the tray. Stanley took the tray and started slowly across the courtyard, in no hurry to get ready for school.

"Eh, Ichiro!" he heard Isaac say as Mateo came in the store. "Don't give this Mateo too much credit! The buggah, he only spend his money for fight chicken."

"Eh, you, Isaac!" Mateo protested, laughing.

When Stanley returned from the house, ready for school, Isaac was gone. Stanley paused for a moment at the top of the driveway with the Wainalii world spread out below him. Ah Fook was sitting on the abandoned pier in the sunshine waiting for the interisland steamer that had stopped calling at Wainalii fifty years ago.

From the village path, Junior and Kimo Kaimana emerged onto the road.

"Hey, Juniah!" yelled Stanley, and ran to catch up with them.

Isaac's visits to the store were never regular, or dependable, but he came often. Afternoons, when his dad was too busy to take off, or his mother was not feeling well enough to be in the store, Stanley did things with Isaac.

Some mornings Isaac came up to spend the first cool half hour of the day with them, drinking coffee and sitting on the bench under the milo tree. Maybe Isaac would feel like talking, and when he did, Stanley and his father listened.

From Isaac, Stanley learned how to look over the water and tell whether a sudden arch of black was shark, or manta ray, dolphin or whale slicing the shining surface of the sea. He heard tales of jumping fireballs, of ghosts, of spirit people who wandered the old coast trails and might be met—Isaac himself had met some—along the mountain road at night. Isaac's stories peopled the empty lands that sloped to the beach on either side of the village and the pier. "Someday!" he promised Stanley. "You and your dad and me, we go *holoholo* all one day up the coast, and I show these things to you!" He talked of secret burial caves where his ancestors' bones were hidden, where there were tattooed mummies, fish-

86

hooks made from human bone, *umeke*—carved wooden bowls inset with human teeth.

From Isaac, Stanley learned the names of the kings and chiefs who had ruled the island in ancient times, a thousand-year-lineage mother to son—for, Isaac explained, a mother is certain. But who one's father is? Who can tell for sure?

Stanley came to know well enough to recite for himself the legends and names and powers of the old Hawaiian gods. Kane. Lono. Kukailimoku. The goddess Pele who ruled over the volcanoes.

Some mornings the three of them sat in a comfortably shared silence, each with his own thoughts, looking down at the beach and the treetops and houses and sea while the cardinals called, "Come here! come here!" and the mynah birds staggered round and round in their ritualistic circles, talking.

"Stanley," said Junior one day on the way to school. "You no miss Chicago? Plenty for do, I bet, in one big place like that!"

Stanley thought for the first time in a long time of his friends back there, and his school, and his old neighborhood. "No," he decided, "more to do in this place, here." He thought hard, bothered by Junior's frown. "It's—it's different," he tried to explain. "In Chicago—well, after school and Saturdays there's nothing to do but go to the Y, or go to the bowling alley, or play kick the can out in the street—"

"Y? What's a Y?" Junior wanted to know.

"What's a bowling alley like?" Kimo asked.

"How do you play kick the can?" said Darwin.

"I like for go see all those things!" said Lester.

Stanley shook his head. "Junk," he said vehemently. "That stuff is all junk. Man, this is real living around here!"

CHAPTER NINE

From Isaac, Stanley learned to spear and dive. Isaac was on the beach one afternoon working on his canoe when Stanley came down.

"Junior, Darwin, Lester, they went out for dive maybe one hour ago. How come you didn't go?"

Stanley shrugged and squinted into the sun. On the ocean side of the reef, where the water changed depth and color, he could see the tips of his friends' snorkels and the bobbing white plastic jug they used to float their string of fish.

"You have mask and fins?" Isaac asked.

"Plenty. In the store. Only I don't know how to use them."

"You can swim okay?"

"I passed junior lifesaving."

Isaac sat back on his heels. "I'll tell you what. You go pick out a mask and fins that fit you. Then stop by my house. Tell Iwalani give you my diving gear. Your papa he's too busy these days so I teach you how we swim in the ocean. Not like one swimming pool! In the ocean, better you always wear mask or goggles. Plenty to see, and plenty you better be careful to see for swim out of their way!"

"Stanley!" Isaac called after him, "Bring one branch of milo leaves with you!"

All the way to the store, and to Isaac's, and back to the beach, Stanley puzzled about why the milo leaves.

"Okay," Isaac approved, checking all that Stanley brought down. He took his mask and the milo branch and walked into the shallow water. Stanley followed, untying the price tag from his new mask.

Isaac sat down in the water, spat into his faceplate, pulled a handful of leaves from the milo branch and handed the branch to Stanley. With some reluctance, Stanley did as Isaac had. He imitated Isaac's tearing the green leaves into strips, wadding them and scouring the spittle around on the glass faceplate, both sides. Next Isaac rinsed the mask in the water, letting the leaves float away. He fitted the

90

rubber rim of the mask to his forehead and upper lip, carefully pulled his hair up out of the way, and pulled the strap down around the back of his head.

"Try," said Isaac, as Stanley fitted his on.

Stanley put his face down in the shallow water. The sea ran in around the sides of the mask, filling it like a cup. Stanley pulled it off, water up his nose and burning his eyes.

"Not tight enough." Isaac helped him adjust the strap. He checked at Stanley's forehead. "If some of your hair catch down inside the rubber, can leak from that." He showed him how to breathe in and let the edges of the mask seal against the skin. "You breathe through your mouth. Never through your nose when you snorkel. In and out. Not fast, not slow."

Stanley floated on his face at the edge of the bay to try. Isaac sluiced a handful of water down the open end of the snorkel tube and Stanley came up choking.

"That's how the waves going hit you, give you water sometime instead of air," said Isaac. "So you always be ready when you breathe in, to fast blow out. Like when you play one bugle." Isaac ran water into his own snorkel. *Pptt-ah!* He blew out a jet of water. "Like so."

He made Stanley practice for a while in the shallow water. "Until you get the feel. Your mask not fogging?"

Stanley shook his head.

"That's the milo juice. If no milo, no naupaka leaves, you can use one cigarette. Rub with tobacco, keeps the glass clear the same way. You never use fins?"

"Once. In the pool."

"Pool?" Isaac shook his head again. "Then, you never learn yet. Come. I show you."

Stanley brought his and Isaac's fins from the sand. "Like so—" Isaac demonstrated. "Like you put on shoes. Now, when you kick, bend the knee! With fins, you make the legs go like you're riding one bicycle. Try!"

Stanley floated face down, kicking fast, the way he had learned in the pool, but trying the pumping bent knee motion of bicycling at the same time.

Isaac motioned for him to stand up. "Not so fast! You tire yourself before you get there. Easy. Slow and easy. Watch!" Isaac slid into the water with the ease of a seal. The tips of his fins never showed. Only the back of his head, the snorkel tube, and the alternate scoop of his arms in a crawl broke the surface.

Stanley tried again. "Hey!" he stood up. "Easier than straight swimming!"

"More easy. Can go faster. Go more far. Stay

longer. Okay. I take you to the reef," said Isaac. "Follow me."

For a long way out, the bay was no more than knee deep.

In deeper water, the bottom changed. There were still pockets and patches of sand, but the bay floor was covered with broken pieces of coral, bleached fragments of shells, broken chunks of water-worn lava.

Stanley and Isaac swam out over coral growing in a profusion of shapes—branching trees, solid brain-like masses, and miniature reefs. The colors of coral intrigued Stanley. Pink. Yellow. Pale blue. Lavendar. They could have waded, but, Stanley realized, that way he would miss the scenery of the shallow water. He liked the intimacy of the smallest creatures a few inches from his face mask. The surprise of a school of baby manini startled out of a bed of sea lettuce. The back end of a crab coming out of a hole. Goaties—strange creatures that looked like a fish but had short stumpy legs so they could either run or swim.

Each of the larger coral heads was like an apartment house. Stanley watched reef fish with sharp beak-shaped mouths working to get food from between the coral branches. There were butterfly fish that looked like their namesakes of the air, dazzling yellows, oranges, striped black and white, sometimes blue. One fish with a pig-shaped snout and crazy-quilt colors had a name he repeated five times and then couldn't get right. *"Humuhumunukunukua-puaa,"* Isaac corrected him.

Stanley noticed how the fish seemed to like to stay in the foaming water where the surf broke against the reef. Inside the reef, the water was perhaps ten feet deep. At the reef, coral grew almost to the surface. Isaac led the way through a pass in the reef that was no more than two canoe lengths wide. Outside the sea bottom was a whole new world again. For a short distance coral and lava sprawled across the rough floor pocketing white sand in holes where the fish seemed to like to congregate. Then, abruptly, a cliff plunged to a depth of fifty feet. Isaac motioned for Stanley to hover and watch at the drop-off. In the clear water that far below, the coral heads looked blue. The cliff face was cut with irregular valleys and great arches and cave mouths. "Watch!" Isaac took a deep breath, jackknifed his body and plummeted down along the face of the cliff. Fish, big ones, less brilliant colors than the small coral and limu feeders of the shallower waters inshore, grazed along like herds of cattle along the drop-off. A river of yellow-and-black-striped fish flowed along feeding in a tight mass on something on the deep coral, then scattered into hundreds of separate shapes as Isaac disturbed them.

94

"You try a dive!" urged Isaac, when he surfaced.

Stanley took a deep breath, jackknifed, and plunged down. Soon, his ears hurt. He liked the feeling of depth, but at the same time he was a little scared. He wondered how far down he had come. What if he hadn't enough air in his lungs left to swim up? The surface and Isaac's floating figure watching him seemed a great distance. Thirty-five feet maybe?

"You got fifteen feet down! Good for first time," said Isaac when Stanley reached the surface. "Remember. Let your breath out slow and easy all the time you're coming up."

From that first time, every afternoon he saw Isaac on the beach Stanley took his mask and fins and went. Once in a while, his dad could come too. Once in a while he and Junior and Kimo and Darwin, maybe Lester Ching, went out by themselves. Best of all Stanley liked the days when he went by himself with Isaac, because those were the days he learned more new things about the sea.

Isaac taught him to spear. It was a good feeling to be able to bring home enough fish for the whole family. He got good enough so that, like Isaac, each time he went out with his spear, he brought back fish. There were days, though, when he left his spear at home and swam out only to look. The fish were,

Isaac insisted, akamai, smart about this. Days when Stanley swam without a spear there were always more fish around, and they did not spook away as he swam by.

In the world above water, there were days when it might be cloudy, rare days when it was cool and overcast, days when it rained. So, too, Stanley discovered, the underwater world had its weather patterns and times of change. Some days he could feel the colder water surging in from the deep ocean. Then the shallows and offshore valleys were murky with clouds of plankton and surf-churned debris. The days when this happened, the fish were different. They paid no attention to him, with or without his spear. The cooler murky water seemed to excite them into playing a kind of wild fish tag, running up to each other, bumping, and quickly darting away. There were days, rare ones, when currents surged in to pull a swimmer from his usual route. But most days, it was clear, warm, and calm, with the sunlight enhancing the rainbow colors of coral and fish, sponge and starfish, and minute anemones.

In a few weeks, he could swim from the beach along routes that had become as familiar to him as the streets between his old neighborhood in Chicago and the downtown Y had once been. He got so he did not have to poke his head out of the water and look back at the shore to be able to know exactly where he was in the bay. He knew which way to swim to be sure not to disturb Isaac's kaku in the shadows of the old pier.

He got so he could dive with ease to thirty feet, but still not like Isaac to fifty and sixty feet. The ledges and cliff faces and valley sides of the drop-off revealed new sights. Sponges, rock scallops, sea weeds, small creatures that looked like spring-operated feathers, dark green starfish the color and spiny texture of cactus. In the crevices hid a variety of shells—tigers and humpbacked cowries, all sizes of cones. The caves, the holes, and archways were shadowy places where, on his slow silver-bubbling way back to the surface, he might glimpse the snaky head of a big eel, jaws opening and closing to show sharp teeth.

"What if a shark should come?" his mother worried whenever he went off to dive, whether it was with Isaac or not.

"Ah! He won't go out that far. Will you, Stanley," his dad reassured.

Stanley was cautious, but because of Isaac's stories and Isaac's attitude, he had dropped his fear of sharks. If one did appear, he would swim away, trying not to attract its attention by too much motion or noise. If one did come too close, Isaac had told him what to do. From Isaac, Stanley had acquired a new feeling for the sea. It was no longer a strange or dangerous place. It was, rather, as natural, as familiar, as safe and comfortable feeling as the pool had been to him in the Chicago Y.

CHAPTER TEN

By summer, it seemed to Stanley that he had always lived as he was now in Wainalii. Time no longer passed as the pages of a month torn from the calendar, or the hours of a day counted from a clock, or the days of the week remembered by what was going to be on the TV a certain night. There were no changes of season, no extremes of hot and cold, wet or dry. There was no sense of living for what might be going to happen some vague hopeful time in the future that might be better, or more exciting, no impatient waiting to be grown-up. He woke up every morning exuberant about the day ahead. He hadn't even counted the days until the end of school.

"You don't mind it here, do you?" his mother

asked one morning when they were in the kitchen alone.

"Mind it?" Stanley stared at her. "I like it! I really like it. I hope I never have to live anyplace else!"

A determined expression of protest crossed her face, like a window opened for Stanley into the thoughts forming in her mind. "Wainalii is not what I want for you though, Stanley. It's not good for you living like this. No—no challenge! You lose your ambition. It's too—too different. You never hear anybody talking about going to college over here, or how important is education, or what they want their children to be."

"Which is exactly why I like it!" Stanley wanted to say. Instead, because he had been brought up not to argue with his mother, he said nothing. He left the kitchen thinking that he could imagine nothing better than to spend the rest of his life living like Isaac, or maybe like his dad, or—best of all—a combination of the two of them.

Vacation made little change in Stanley's days. He prowled the beach alone as it grew light. If Isaac had been night fishing, he helped unload and clean the canoe. If Isaac was going out morning fishing, he helped him get ready. Always Isaac invited him to go along. Always, so far, whenever Stanley asked, his father found some excuse to say no.

"That's all right. Someday. Some one of these days!" Isaac promised. "You and me we go out all night and all day in my canoe, and I teach you to sail."

At six-thirty, same as on school mornings, Stanley was home and eating breakfast. He helped open the store. If Isaac were up for coffee, he listened to the talk. No rush, that was the difference in summertime. He chose his own pace of work. All that mattered was it got done.

On Mondays and Thursdays, he left at nine with his father to take up the mail. The twice weekly trips with the mail sack, the box of stamps, petty cash, and post cards in the post office end of the store, had become the most important part of their business.

"If it weren't for the post office, we couldn't afford to stay in Wainalii," his dad admitted to him one morning. "If we can just hang on. Even for one year! I tell your mother. Be patient. Give the place a chance." He sighed, sounding so discouraged that from then on Stanley began to lie awake at night, trying to figure out ways to keep them living in Wainalii.

Their secondhand truck was not in the best condition. Neither was the narrow road that climbed to the ranch town where there was a pick up for branch post offices from this end of the island. The mail went out in one of the interisland planes that serviced the small airport with regularly scheduled flights to Honolulu. There was a truck station where they could pick up what supplies they ordered by phone from Hilo wholesalers. There was a vegetable stand where they bought fresh produce, eggs, and milk. The ranch town was one business strip along the highway, less than three city blocks in length, with plenty of open land between the scattered buildings. To Stanley, on each successive trip, the town of fourteen hundred people looked more like a metropolis.

He looked forward to these summer Mondays and Thursdays. With every mile the road climbed from Wainalii, the temperature grew cooler. Elevation changed the kiawe and sparse sunburned grass to cactus and grazing land and occasional big gnarled trees, remnants of the forest Isaac had said once covered these slopes.

There were usually cowboys riding their horses along the highway. There was a hitching rack at the post office and at the ranch general store. Some mornings when the mist blew down off the hills, Stanley felt as cold helping load the cartons of canned goods and cases of soda as he remembered feeling on raw spring days in Chicago when he took off his winter jacket too soon.

"Goes fast when you're along to help!" his dad complimented. The rounds from post office to freight station, to the airport for the bundle of newspapers, to the vegetable stand, and then to the coffee shop to wait for the mail truck to come from Hilo took two hours. "Good place to catch up on the news," Ichiro grinned as he and Stanley walked in the first summer morning they made the trip. "Only one sweet roll Stanley? Nothing to drink? You sure?"

Stanley pretended the sweet roll and a glass of water were enough. He tried to spend as little money as possible. The further he could help stretch their dollars, the longer he figured they'd be able to live in Wainalii. By one o'clock they were home. They ate lunch. Stanley helped unload the truck. After that, he was free. He swam. He dived. He hunted shells. He hung around helping Isaac. Junior and Kimo were sent to Honolulu to stay with relatives for the vacation. Darwin Pahanui was with relatives in Puna for July. Lester Ching was staying up at the ranch, but, with Isaac, Stanley didn't miss his friends.

There was not that much work in the store to keep him busy the days they didn't make the trip for supplies and mail. Isaac noticed this. So, one morning he came up early, before six. "Stanley," he proposed, "today I'm going walk up the coast and go throw net. Maybe I come back late this afternoon. How about you come with me? You too, Ichiro, if you can get away."

Stanley hesitated, a yes on his tongue but his eyes on his dad. The way Isaac asked, directly of him

103

and not through his father, pleased him. It was getting harder and harder to ask every time to do something which he figured anyway, now he was fourteen, he ought to be able to decide for himself.

"I finished the storeroom yesterday when we got back," Stanley volunteered. "And the truck is cleaned out." He waited impatiently for his dad to say something.

"Can, or cannot Stanley," said Isaac.

Stanley turned to his dad.

"Why not?" said Ichiro. "I'd like to go myself. Stanley, quick. Go get Momma to pack you a lunch."

"No need!" Isaac said. "Just go eat your breakfast. I wait for you at my house. You come down."

Stanley raced to the kitchen. He put his scrambled eggs between two pieces of toast for a sandwich to eat on the way.

"But his milk! And no fruit!" he could hear his mother calling him back, complaining to his father.

"Let him go, Sueko!"

Stanley took half the sandwich in one hungry bite and bolted down to Isaac's.

They took the trail that led through the kiawes, past the kapu beach, and south into the kiawe forest that hugged the coast. The air was still and hot. Doves flew up from branches overhead at their approach. Wild pigs rustled through the thorny tangles of trees blown down or split from age. Every now and then a branch rubbed creaking limb against limb in an oddly human sound. Cattle flies clustered on Stanley's head, back, forearms, and face. He kept whisking them away with a switch of green kiawe. Isaac did not seem bothered. He let the flies land on his mouth, crawl around inside the edges of his nostrils, and sit on the back of his neck in such numbers that just to look at them made Stanley itchy.

Along the trail were glimpses of stone walls hidden by the kiawe, of stone platforms and overgrown pathways, and relics Isaac pointed out as they passed. An hour's walk and they came to low flat coastline, lava tongues that were the edges of a smooth pahoehoe flow stretching in peninsulas into the sea. Between the tongues of pahoehoe, and caught in low spots in the lava, were tide pools alive with small fish, some with wana and sea cucumbers and small corals.

Sandpipers skittered over the hot black lava and white coral sand pockets of the tide flats. Seabirds hovered offshore in low skimming circles of flight above the white curds of the surf. Black crabs roved sideways along the crevices of the lava. Their claws were busy, picking and eating, until a shadow or footfall startled them, and they plunged into the nearest hiding place. "We wait for one special place to throw net," said Isaac. "Two more villages, then there's a good moi hole."

105

In those last two villages there had been people living until not too long ago. "In my time yet," said Isaac. Haole style houses were built on the old stone platforms. They passed half a dozen of them, wall boards torn off, steps and posts missing, where someone had helped himself to firewood. The framing and walls that remained were being turned to dust by termites and carpenter bees.

Stanley recognized some of the names that welled up from Isaac's memory to identify the shacks that were left or the platforms that had been house foundations. The families had moved to Wainalii, or Isaac had mentioned them in his stories of relatives and oldtimers who left this coast to move to Honolulu or to the mainland in the great exodus for jobs the last thirty years.

They passed a Hawaiian mission church bigger than the one in Wainalii. Its coral cement walls were still standing. The roof was gone. There were holes in the walls where door and window frames had once hung. The pews and pulpit were termite eaten so that what wood remained looked like Swiss cheese.

"One hundred years ago, they built this, and it's broken down—nobody here to use for how long now? But the heiau—you been with Junior up to the old Hawaiian temple past the schoolhouse yet? No? Someday I take you! More than one thousand years old and still each stone in place like it was from those

times! It outlast this. It outlast the church at Wainalii. They close up that one finally last year."

Isaac paused in the graveyard of the church. He
uprooted seedling kiawes from some of the graves.
He straightened the rows of coral and beach-stone
markers. He set up the overturned jelly jars of dried
flowers. "Pretty soon," he grumbled, "there won't be
anybody left who knows who these people were.

"By the time you come old like me, maybe no
graveyard left even," said Isaac gloomily. "I don't
like what I read in the papers, Stanley. I don't like
what I hear on the radio. Progress, they call it. More
tourists. More hotels. No place looking like it used
to. Coast haoles moving here to live. Yesterday they
told on the radio about a road they like to build along
this coast." Isaac looked melancholy. "It's coming,
that road, Stanley. But I'm hoping not in my life-
time. Honolulu, too late already for keep it like it
used to be. Hilo, they need the business. Wainalii,
we don't want anything different. We don't need
one road running through with everybody coming
down to look at us, and spoil our fishing grounds."
Isaac doubled his pace. Stanley jogged to keep up
with him.

When they stopped, Isaac said, "The trail goes
on. All the way to Kona. This place, this is where
I like try throw net today."

Stanley set down the lauhala shoulder basket he

107

had carried. The next point, the next bay, a flash of distant white sand beach, an isolated palm grove ahead, intrigued him. He'd have liked to keep on, to walk all the way to Kona now.

The reef was a distance offshore. A deep slit pierced it in a vee of blue against the surrounding green shallow water. "Always plenty of fish hang around there," said Isaac, pointing to the slit.

Between the beach and the reef was a maze of channels and lava islets. Big broken chunks of coral showed the hollow tombs of sea worms inside. Pockets of green and black sand were along the beach. The tide pools closest to them had an oily appearance. "Fresh water springs in them, that's why." Isaac stooped and put his mouth against an oily-looking seepage. "Try!"

Stanley bent and tried. The water was brackish but drinkable. They left their water jug against the bleached skeleton of a dead kiawe on the beach. Then, no conversation as they went, they walked out to the reef.

On the way, Isaac had carried the heavy throw net on his shoulders. Now he gathered it into long even folds—a third of the circular hand-tied, weighted net held close to his body with his left hand, a third suspended from his right hand, and the remainder flung over his shoulder. He approached the water's edge with the careful crouching motion of a cat stalking a bird.

"Never let your shadow fall on the water when you go for throw net," he cautioned. Stanley followed Isaac, imitating his every motion. Isaac's huge body had the lightness and grace of a dancer's as he stalked. He held the net ready, looking into the water with an oblique stare as if in this way his eyes could pierce the sunstruck blue lens of the surface and see the darting colors and shapes of the fish below. Four waves came in and broke and ran in white foam up and over the lava walls of the slit in the reef before he straightened. The fifth wave crashed in. In one swift motion, Isaac flung the net up and out. The coarse mesh netted the sunlight. It dropped, in a perfect circle, into the water. Before the foaming from the breaker stopped, Isaac plunged to gather the net.

Stanley came running. Trapped in the net, silvery as the water sluicing off the cords, were a dozen fish. Stanley plucked them from the net and into his lauhala hamper. Isaac regathered his net, crouched again, and walked on to another place to wait for the next school of fish.

In an hour, the lauhala basket was filled. Stanley could just manage to carry it; the leather straps cutting into his shoulders from the load. They ate raw fish, island style, for their lunch. Then Isaac lay in the shade of a kiawe and fell asleep. Stanley lay gazing at the ocean, waiting for Isaac to wake up until he fell asleep himself.

On the walk home, they saw a sea turtle swimming along close to the shore. A floating log deceived them for a few minutes into thinking they saw a small boat on the horizon. "Good place to fish, near one of these floating logs," said Isaac. "Underneath, it's covered with limu, seaweed. That's where the small mahimahi like to feed. Ah, Stanley. I tell you! Next time we come *holoholo* all day in my canoe. We go for a big fish out in the channel. Okay?"

"Okay!" said Stanley. He wished he could go like this with Isaac all day every day.

They were halfway home when a helicopter clattered into view. It hovered above them like some monstrous dragonfly. Stanley waved and ran out on the lava flat to look up into the Plexiglass body at the pilot and two passengers.

"Look, Isaac. Look! First time I ever saw one so close! I'd like a ride in one of those," he wished aloud. "Look, Isaac! They're taking pictures. Of us!"

Isaac did not wave. He stared up with a sober expression at the noisy rotors of the machine. All day, all along the coast, they had not seen another person, not even a sign of a boat on the sea. Only the

110

noon Hawaiian Air Lines' jet flying high overhead toward Kona had disturbed them. Isaac scowled at the helicopter. "I don't like this kind starting to come poke around looking down into every place along here," he complained. "They scare the fish."

He turned and watched as the helicopter went on up the coast. It hovered lower and lower in its awkward-looking fashion until it settled to land on the same lava flat from which, before lunch, Isaac had netted fish. "Look. You see that?" he complained to Stanley. "They scare all the fish away. A helicopter. I ask you. What for's a helicopter coming around here?"

CHAPTER ELEVEN

The next afternoon the helicopter came racketing down off the mountainside to Wainalii.

"I told you! It's the one we saw yesterday." Stanley raced to the edge of the courtyard, looking up. His mother came from the store, her face upturned, watching the whirling rotors and saying, "Oh, oh, oh!" in a dazed, excited voice. "Ichiro! Girls! Ba-chan! Come see!"

Sheryl and Louise hung onto their father, shrieking with excitement, half-scared. Ba-chan hustled down from her work in the kitchen, a rice-sack dish towel in one hand, the other clapped over her mouth to hide the fact that in her excitement she had left her false teeth in the cup on the drainboard where

112

she usually kept them when she was in the house alone.

Stanley hesitated at the top of the drive.

"Go!" Ichiro urged. "We all go. I lock the store. Sheryl—Louise. You wait for me!"

Stanley raced down the driveway trying to keep up with the chopper. It hovered briefly over the palm grove, then sidled down to land on the beach between the park and the village canoes.

From their houses, from two canoes ready to push off across the shallow waters of the bay, from up the beach where Queenie and Emma Ching and Mrs. Pahanui had been picking wana, all of Wainalii erupted onto the beach, each one jostling as close as he could to the landing whirlybird.

The same two men in visored caps whom Stanley had waved to yesterday climbed out of the machine. One had binoculars and several cameras in carrying cases. The other carried a bundle of rolled maps.

"Eh. You make movies? Make pictuah for telewision?" asked the youngest Kainoa, who was never afraid to ask questions of anyone.

Stanley ran to stand with Isaac who was at the front of the crowd.

"You look for something or somebody?" Isaac accosted the two men. "You tourists?"

The two men hesitated. They had the polite embarrassed expressions of strangers who are not understanding what they hear. "Tourists? Well—not really," said the elder of the two. They both reminded Stanley of vaguely familiar faces in the TV—handsome, suntanned, one blond and the other with gray hair, each with sunglasses and very white teeth and big smiles. He was relieved when his father stepped forward, hand extended in welcome. "Sasaki. Ichiro Sasaki. I'm postmaster here. We never had a helicopter land in Wainalii so that's why we're all so curious. We can help you with anything? Take you around the village? You like to come up to my store for a cold drink?"

"Or my house. Come my house! Get cold beer!" Yama Ching added. There was a stir of invitations. From Mateo. From Moses Ii. From Mr. Pahanui. From the Kainoas's. The Alapais's. Only Isaac held aloof from the instant welcome that now surged out to the strangers.

"I'm Dave Champion," said the gray-haired man. "My assistant here, Peter Whiteridge. Resco." The two men shook hands all around, going from one person to the other in such a direct, friendly way that Stanley was ashamed of Isaac for holding back and standing aloof to one side.

"I have never seen a more beautiful place," said the younger man. "Dave, you can have all that lava up along the coast. I'll take this. Look at the beach!"

"Come. Come up to my store. Beautiful view. And a cold drink!" Stanley was proud of the way his father took over, making the strangers feel at home. Resco, he puzzled. He'd heard that name, but he couldn't remember where.

"Resco?" Ichiro, leading the two men through the palm grove was caught by that name too.

"We're a California-based firm. Resort development," Mr. Champion smiled. "Diversified, with interests in Australia and the Philippines and Central America. We've expanded to Hawaii this year."

Stanley looked back. Everyone was following them to the store. Even Isaac. He ran to bring two chairs from the house for the two men. His father and Isaac and Yama Ching sat on the bench. Stanley fetched cold beer for the two visitors, beer for his father and Yama, orange soda for Isaac. Isaac didn't touch his. He sat saying nothing, looking suspicious.

"Resco," said Yama, when they were all comfortable, and the two strangers had had the chance to admire and photograph the view. "That's the outfit building the new hotel on Maui?"

Mr. Champion nodded.

"The one has a resort coming up on Kauai too?" asked Stanley's father.

Mr. Champion nodded again.

"Dave," said Mr. Whiteridge, "it won't be priviledged information after the newspapers and radio get hold of the news in the next day or two. So why not tell these good people before they read about the deal?"

"Why not. Good idea, Pete!" Mr. Champion was enthused. He slid the rubber bands off the map rolls and spread the maps out on his knees.

"Wainalii!" Stanley read the legend by looking over Mr. Champion's shoulder. "Only—only—"

"Only it's not the Wainalii that you can see by looking down from here today!" Mr. Champion laughed. "This map is a projection of our plans for the resort Resco intends to develop here."

"Here? Where?" interrupted Isaac.

"Oh—the whole beach. All along below from the park boundary to the lighthouse point. And we may be able to exchange lands to acquire the park piece, too. We hope. Looks as if we'll have to blast out that old pier. Too far gone to rebuild for the charter boats we intend to keep tied up alongside."

Yama Ching scratched his head with the mouth of his empty beer bottle. "Resort? From the park to the lighthouse? But that's where the village is. That's where all of us live!" He frowned. "You got your map wrong, I think. All of us, we're on—well, we're—we've always lived down here!"

Mr. Champion looked as polite and enthused as if he were giving out pleasant information. Stanley listened, his eyes on Isaac, liking the strangers less and less with each word. "The only land in Wainalii not owned by your state government is Mr. Sasaki's six acres. He can sell or choose not to sell to us. We don't care. Our option is on the state lands. He has the only land fee simple."

"Not so!" contradicted Isaac. "My land is mine from my grandmother to me."

"No title on file in the bureau of conveyances. No designation on the tax maps. The village is all state land. We now hold the option on it. Our agreement with your state government, however, was that Resco will bear all and any expense of relocating your homes to a subdivision on the bluff beyond the lighthouse, with each of you being entitled to a house lot of twelve thousand square feet. Our impression is that this is most generous, considering."

Mr. Champion handed the map to Stanley's father. Stanley stared at it as his dad held it up and out so Yama and Isaac could see. Three hotels and a golf course were sketched in an artist's rendition where the village now lay. There was a marina at the abandoned pier, a heliport on the lighthouse point. The six acres of the store was a blank red area.

Stanley saw his mother and father exchange astonished glances. He looked at Isaac and at Yama. For everyone in the village except his own family, Stanley realized, what was drawn on this map was a catastrophe.

The two strangers seemed oblivious to the sudden quiet and the change in mood of everyone around. They talked, the two of them by turns, exclaiming over all the advantages of the site. "As a matter of fact," Mr. Champion's forefinger reached over to travel along the map, "location of the new village, a waterline into Wainalii, and the new road from the airport are going to be phase one of this development. The state is being most supportive. The legislature paved the way by appropriations which can be used for the road and the waterline. For Resco's part, I feel sure we will be starting site preparation down here this fall." He looked around, his expression confident.

"As usual with a Resco development, we hope to sign up you local people for construction jobs and train you later for jobs in the hotels. Local people get priority, that's our motto. I must say we are very pleased with the area here at Wainalii. The deal has gone much more quickly and easily than we had anticipated. It's been kept pretty quiet, of course. We didn't want any competition coming in! The press will be given the announcement of all I've told you today by—well, say Friday, Pete?" His companion nodded and gave all the sober faces a big smile.

"What was it you said about our six acres?" asked Stanley's mother.

Mr. Champion answered. "You're fee simple.

If we want your acreage, we'll have to buy it from you. Or—we may suggest that you maintain your store if you don't choose to sell. You may want to expand your business. Change more to a resort shop clientele. I'd think a local store like this, though, would keep some atmosphere for our hotel guests, right, Pete?"

"Local color. Preserve the island flavor. "Capitalize on the natural assets. That's our aim!" said Mr. Whiteridge. He reminded Stanley of a salesman advertising toothpaste or laundry detergent on TV.

"Like," said Mr. Champion, "Resco would encourage the hotel management to allow you people to keep your canoes on the beach."

"Big deal!" Isaac interrupted him.

Mr. Champion laughed and then, sensing the reaction around the courtyard, he stopped laughing and shrugged. Mr. Whiteridge took the map and rerolled it.

"But ours is ours? No problem?" Stanley's mother repeated.

"No problem, Mrs. Sasaki," assured Mr. Champion. He looked at her with interest. Hers had become the only friendly face in the crowd.

Isaac got up and left, saying nothing. Mr. Champion and Mr. Whiteridge walked back down to the helicopter. Slowly, without any conversation, everyone followed.

Ba-chan began picking up empty soda bottles, one hand cupped over her toothless mouth. Stanley stayed in the courtyard, listening to his parents and feeling queer. He shushed Sheryl and Louise who were badgering him to take them to see the helicopter fly away.

"Hotel. Resort! Oh, Ichiro! And I never believed you before!" Stanley's mother exclaimed. "We do have it made. You were right. How lucky! How good for us!"

"Only," said Ichiro, "I don't like the way they're going about it to upset everybody else."

Upset? That was hardly the word. They can't! Stanley thought indignantly. Isaac was right!

He knew he should go help his grandmother clean the courtyard. He knew he should take Sheryl and Louise down to see the helicopter leave. He felt like neither. He just stood there thinking of how it was going to be the way the artist showed with three hotels and a golf course—and, he'd noticed, the golf course wound around to include the kiawes and the clearing where the shark stone stayed behind the kapu beach. He turned his back on the view. His mother was radiant, transfigured, different, and happier than he ever remembered seeing her before. No problem now. They had it made here.

No need now to worry at night. No need to have only a sweet roll and water when he was so hungry in the coffee shop on their trips. Potential, his dad had always daydreamed aloud. Potential. Stanley had never understood what a two-edged terrible word that might be.

CHAPTER TWELVE

He woke that night with the noise of the wind. The edge of a roofing tin flapped loose. A metal ashtray blew off the table next to the couch that was his bed in the living room.

Outside, a door began banging open and shut, open and shut. Stanley got up, hunted a flashlight, and went down the porch steps in his pajamas to find the source of the noise. He had been having such crazy dreams he was glad to be wakened. Dreams about the two haole men and their maps. About Isaac's quiet rage. The villagers' stunned faces. His mother's jubilance. The clearing with the shark stone wrecked by bulldozers. The dreams kept floating in his mind, so vivid they had the tinge of reality. He shook them off, wishing he could do the same with everything that had happened today.

It gave him an odd good feeling of independence to be up, alone, and out in the middle of the night.

Two minutes' search, and he'd found the banging door. It was the one to the bathhouse. He propped it shut with a rock so it wouldn't blow open and start banging again. He stood listening to the gusts, strong and warm, blowing from the southwest. Kona wind, he knew from Isaac's descriptions of it. The kona wind was the storm wind of Wainalii.

The courtyard was already littered with small branches and milo leaves. The bench was over-turned. Stanley set it up again and then checked the storefront. Everything okay. He nodded, feeling important. He wasn't sleepy. He switched off the flashlight and stood in the courtyard looking at the clouds that were moving by. Great patches of stars were intermittently blotted from view. The surf was noisy against the reef. High tide, he surmised. He stood at the top of the driveway, looking out over the village. There was a light on in Isaac's house. As he watched, the door filled with Isaac's silhouette. Trouble? Stanley wondered. Maybe, if the wind were going to pick up and the ocean get rough at high tide like this, Isaac would want to move his canoe to a safer place. Without a look or thought back at the house, Stanley ran down the drive and after the moving halo of lantern light accompanying Isaac through the grove.

He waited, bracing himself by holding to a coconut tree as an extraordinary gust of wind roared past. The slender trunk whipped into a curve. A barrage of ripe coconuts hurtled from high overhead, just missing him in the darkness.

"Auwe!" said Stanley. He raced to get out from under the trees, calling to Isaac. The noise of the surf drowned his voice. This close the sea sounded like a dozen freight trains converging all at once to crash against the reef. The sea foamed in swirls above the high-tide mark. Stanley could taste the salt spray. "Isaac!" he yelled.

Isaac turned, the lantern held high in one hand, the other poised over the last roofing tin that shielded his canoe. "Eh. Stanley! What you doing up?"

Stanley turned off his flashlight and stuck it into the waistband of his pajamas. "I saw your light. I figured maybe you need some help."

"Ah. You came for *kokua* me. Too good, you Stanley. Thanks, eh?" He handed Stanley the lantern. "Hold this for me."

Stanley held it while Isaac removed the last roofing tin, set the mast, checked the sail, the anchor, the steering paddle, the bailer, and water jug.

"You're not going out!" Stanley gasped. He glanced at the noisy blackness of the bay. He listened

124

to the gusts of wind coming. A big one scooped up part of the beach and scoured his face with sand. His eyes stung. His teeth felt gritty. "Aaaaaah!" he spat. "Too rough, Isaac. Not in this wind!"

Isaac laughed. "Hold the lantern!" he admonished. A hot slamming gust nearly tore it from Stanley's hand. He had to dig his toes into the sand to keep from being blown off his feet. In the calm interval following the gust, Isaac pulled the canoe down over the beach.

"Too rough, Isaac!" Stanley protested, coming along with the lantern.

"No scare. Good for sailing, this kona wind." He slid the canoe into the foaming rough edge of the bay. "Us go?" he invited. "My head stay tired from all the pilikia those haoles bring to us today. I have to get out on the sea and think, Stanley."

Stanley hesitated. "Long time now you tell me you go for a sail with me one night."

Stanley looked up at his dark house, knowing if he went he should ask first, or anyway leave a note about where he had gone. He looked at Isaac.

"You scare?"

Stanley blew out the lantern. To be scared, either here or in Chicago, was to be chicken, and chicken was something that, at this instant, Stanley made up his mind not to be. He waded out. The waves sucked the sand bottom into miniature banks against his feet with such force that he could scarcely keep his balance. They'll never know I went, he promised. Two o'clock now? Maybe not that late yet. Before dawn, Isaac usually came home.

"No burn yourself on that lantern. Give it to me," Isaac directed. He put the lantern in the bow. Stanley climbed in amidships. Isaac walked the canoe out to where water swirled around his thighs. Then he got in the stern, digging the paddle into the surging water and hoisting the sail. It was like flying when the wind pushed past them against the tightening canvas, and the canoe rushed into the blackness. Stanley took one quick look back. "Auwe!" he thought. It was too late to change his mind.

"No stand up now!" Isaac shouted.

Stanley hunched into the bottom of the canoe, holding with all his strength to the gunwhales, scared, exhilarated, shivering with excitement and cold wet spray. The yellow sail was light against the blackness. The surf pounded and solid water dashed into the canoe as they shot out through the channel entrance.

"Bail!" yelled Isaac.

Stanley bailed while the waves rose and fell in sickening gulfs and crests of blackness. Gusts of wind screamed past.

"No scare!" Isaac reassured.

The spray wetting his face, the receding black mass of the coastline, the heaving dark sea around

126

him, the increasing strength of the wind, made Stanley feel suddenly ill.

"You like it?" Isaac asked.

"I like it!" Stanley managed to answer. I'm not really lying he apologized to that inner voice of his that was always aghast when he didn't tell the truth. Sick as he was, he liked this lifting, rushing quiet motion of sailing. Only maybe better in the daylight. And not in a Kona storm.

Stanley hung his head over the gunwhales, vomiting until there was nothing left but a dry heave. He lay in the bottom of the canoe, dizzy, sweaty, weak, and most of all—ashamed.

"Feel better?" said Isaac in a gentle voice. "You'll be okay. First time, for plenty people, they get used to the sea like that."

Stanley had no notion how long he slept. When he woke, the wind was still strong, but steady. The clouds had moved on. Stars crowded the sky. He sat up, no longer queasy, and looked around. The island was a dark, distant silhouette. There was the intermittent wink of a lighthouse that might have been Wainalii Light.

"Come. You sail her," said Isaac. "I teach you how."

The feeling of the canoe was lightness and speed. The rush of wind past the sail, the pull of the steering oar as Isaac showed him how to use it as a rudder, how to trim the sail by taking in or letting out on the line that controlled the angle of the boom. Stanley's arms ached after a short time at the steering paddle. His fingers chafed under the strain of the manila lines Isaac called sheets. His hands were numb when he changed places with Isaac to rest for a while. At intervals until dawn, Stanley practiced and rested, practiced and rested, and, as he rested, he sat listening to Isaac recite the Hawaiian names for the constellations overhead, and the Hawaiian names for the winds that prevailed along this coast. Isaac told him the legends of stars that had once guided the sailing canoes of ancient times back and forth between Hawaii and the Great Southern Sea.

It was still dark when Stanley dozed off. He woke with the sun in his face. He sat up, moving suddenly. They were nowhere near shore, nor near anyplace that looked like Wainalii. I shouldn't have come, he thought with panic.

"Easy!" cautioned Isaac. "In a sailing canoe you only move easy—always you shift your weight so the balance is just right. By and by—you'll learn so you know just when, and how, and which way. Look where we are, Stanley! She get up and go in this wind, I tell you! We travel last night! You learn fast how to sail. Take her again now?"

Stanley felt the warmth of pleasure at Isaac's praise. He decided not to worry about what would

128

happen when he got back. It might be a long while before they let him come out with Isaac like this again. He blinked at the surrounding horizon of ocean and distant land and sky. They were far offshore. The mountains and bays and green smudges of palm grove, the black scars of lava, the distant shapes that might be buildings on the beach, were certainly not Wainalii.

"You don't know where we are," smiled Isaac. "You never was this place before. You see the palm trees on the beach? My grandmother who raised me, her father came from that place. Kiholo. No village left now but ah, the nice place for one!" Isaac frowned. "Kiholo. Nobody there. Nobody in their way. How come they don't put their hotel on the government lands in Kiholo and leave us alone at Wainalii!"

Stanley gazed with curiosity at the shore. He was eager to see that place, to see all the places that Isaac and the canoe might take him.

"You miss it in the night though, when you were sleeping. You didn't hear him? I almost woke you up, only—" Isaac sounded excited. "You heard the whales later maybe? After he left us. The whales play close to the boat. Slap their tails on the water. Come up and blow—ho, the stink!"

"He?"

Isaac nodded. "He. Somebody I never told you

129

about before." He pointed and for an instant Stanley dreaded to have to look. "There. Out there. No, not him this time. The whales again." Isaac smiled at the way the expression changed on Stanley's face and the eagerness with which he turned to see. Two great shiny backs arched out of the water and disappeared under twin spouts of spray that smoked high into the clear air. "No good if they come too close to us. They could capsize the canoe. You hungry, Stanley? I can catch a fish if you like eat."

"Not hungry," said Stanley.

"I should have waked you maybe to see him. You—you must be good luck," said Isaac. "First time in all the years I search for him, he come to me! You can't imagine how he looked. So beautiful. A red shark!"

"Red shark!" Stanley protested. "No such thing as a red shark, Isaac. I read all about sharks in the two encyclopedias in school."

"You believe everything what somebody wrote down and printed on a piece of paper? Aaaaaah, Stanley! Open your mind! I don't know how many red shark there are except him. Maybe he's the only one. Special one! No ordinary shark, Stanley. He's red color because his grandmother, and my grandmother—her father came from the village used to be at Kiholo—she was what Hawaiians call *ehu*, means she had reddish hair. Her father, he was *ehu* Hawai-

130

ian before her. Maybe three, four hundred years ago, a Spanish ship get wrecked off Napoopoo, the Kona coast. The Spanish captain, and one wahine supposed to be his sister, the two of them rescued by the village people in their canoes. The rest, they all drown. Redheaded the both of them, that Spanish captain and his sister. They stay with the Kona people. They marry Hawaiian wife, Hawaiian husband. The children, both sides, they get red hair, and my grandmother's father, he came from one of those families. You notice the reddish hair on my Junior? That's why my brother, too, he's a red shark."

Stanley sat rigid, gooseflesh roughening his skin, chills quivering through him. "Brother!" he protested.

"I tell you the story," said Isaac. "Then you, my friend's son, you going to know more than my own sons know. I tell you because you listen to me. Because you believe all what I tell you. Because you, inside, you more like my own, like me. I make up my mind last night when he came to talk to me, Stanley. I *hanai* you. I tell you all what I know, all! When I am gone, in my place you be *kahu* for the shark stone. You care for him and you care for my brother the red shark. And someday, Stanley, you be *kahu* for me. You promise me this?"

"For—for you? Why *kahu* for you, Isaac?"

Isaac shrugged. "I don't know. I never make up

131

my mind yet, but—" He looked out at the sea in a strange, terrifying way. "You will, if need, Stanley? You promise me?"

Reluctantly, Stanley nodded.

"The first day you were here, the morning you went inside the clearing and the shark stone let you see him in his power, that was the sign. That's why I ask you this. That's why I teach to you all I know. That's why I decide, Stanley. I *hanai* you. From now, you are like my own son. More close to me than my own."

Stanley could not wrench his eyes from Isaac's.

"Maybe something, some blood tie between us two in the past," said Isaac. His gesture embraced the shoreline, the great green waves, the blue arch of the sky, the diminished wind curving the yellow sail. "Maybe because you and me, we have the same kind *mana*, the same kind—I don't know what you call it in English but there it is, whatever it is, *mana*. You are my kind inside you, Stanley. You have the same kind inner power. Now I tell you what I never told one person since my grandmother tell this to me. I tell you who he is, and what he is, and why I have searched for him always in my canoe, and why it is another sign that last night, with you along, he came to me."

Stanley hugged his knees, shivering in the sunshine. Like the shark-stone story, this was something

132

he wanted to hear and yet was almost afraid to listen to. A stone who was a shark. A red shark brother. His imagination boggled. Could not be, he kept insisting, but as he listened, the small inner voice of his intuition told him such things might be. Who knew?

"One day," said Isaac, "before I was born my mother and father lived up the coast about five miles past where we went to throw the net. They had a shack all to themselves. Good beach. Plenty fish in the ocean. A few coconut trees. No near neighbors. Once a week they sail to Wainalii, or they paddle, if no wind or wrong wind, which can happen around here. They were young then, first married. My father was caretaker for one rich old haole man had a summer house there. The old man came over from Honolulu maybe one or two times a year. So easy job.

"That first year my mother got big in the belly with her first baby. One morning my father was fixing the canoe to go to Wainalii for supplies like they do every week when my mother say to him that her time has come. Early, maybe too early she think, but no can help. Once it start, the baby has to come out.

"So my father carry the canoe up out of the water again. He went with my mother inside their shack. Not long, they wait. The baby came fast. My mother is right. Too early. Six-months baby. No hair yet. No fingernail. A small little baby born like that cannot live.

"Auwe. Their first one. A boy. You can imagine how sad they feel. 'I think he is dead. So, better we go for our supply anyway in the canoe,' my mother say to my father. 'No more cracker, no more poi, nothing left inside our house for eat.' The ocean is okay to travel that day but it is the season you cannot tell. One day calm. Next day, white water and bad current and high wind.

"As soon as my mother feel more strong, around noontime, they wrap up the little dead baby in one of her muumuu. They hide it down in a puka in one big rock to cover it all over so nothing can get at it before they come home. When they get back from Wainalii, my father promise to my mother, then they make nice grave for their poor little dead new baby, close to the corner of their shack. That was Hawaiian custom, old days after people stopped using burial caves. They bury their dead close by, close to the family, somewhere in the house yard. (That's why, Stanley, not too many graves for all the people used to live in Wainalii.)

"They don't hurry, but they don't waste time on their trip. You know how us Hawaiians are. When they reach Wainalii, they go first thing to my grandmother's house. They tell her about the baby. They all sit around and cry. My grandmother makes prayer,

Christian prayer, because my mother is strong Christian, no listen to my grandmother tell of the old ways.

"Late in the day they kiss my grandmother goodbye. Everybody's face is wet and sad. Then they hurry up to the store for buy what they need. They load up. They sail for home out of the bay. By now, funny kind weather out in the ocean. The sky is all puka puka with cloud. Big swell on the sea. They figure better they go anyway, but halfway home a squall catch up to them. The wind blow and stop, *kapulu* way in circles—slam, slam, slam! Lucky for them they are offshore their place before the wind and waves pile up and capsize them.

"Rain. Ah, rain they tell to my grandmother afterward, so much rain you think the earth turn upside down and all the other six ocean run across the sky and down on top of their heads. They grab hold of the canoe. They swim with it to the beach. *Poho* though, they lose the cracker, the corned beef, the poi. Strong swimmers those two, and so busy in all the rain getting themselves and the canoe inside that my mother never notice something until my father tell her about it when they crawl out on the beach.

" 'Auwe!' says my father. 'Lucky for us, your family have shark for aumakua. They follow us almost inside here, plenty big shark!'

" 'You are worse than my mother to say such old-fashion Hawaiian kind things,' my mother scold him. 'Shark don't bother us because we swim inside too fast.'

" 'Ah, I don't know though!' my father says. He is like my grandmother. He's heard. He believes.

"They turn the canoe rightside in the shallow water, carry it up to the usual place. Then they hurry inside the shack. All this time, the hard rain is coming down. They hurry for put buckets and calabashes all around on the floor to catch the water pouring through the leaky places in the roof.

"The hard rain lasts until dark. The moon coming out from the edge of the clouds, and only that much light when my father and mother go outside to do what they want to do since first they came swimming in for their lives with their canoe. Nighttime, sure, but my mother is anxious to make one grave for the baby. My father brings the lantern. In the lantern light, by the front corner of the house, he starts to dig a hole in the wet ground. All cinders and coral sand their place, so the rainwater doesn't stand around on the ground for long. In the moonlight, my mother goes to get the baby they left in the muumuu under the rock. Only, when she go to get him—no more! She cry out to my father. 'Auwe! He is gone!'

"The both of them look and look and study the ground because maybe, they think first, the big rain

136

come down and wash out that place and carry the body into the sea. But no sign of runoff, or washout, only standing water in the hollows of some big lava boulders close by.

"With the lantern, they search all over. Up and down the beach. Back into the hala forest. All around the rich old man's beach house. No baby— no trace, no sign of that flowered muumuu and what they put under it.

"All night they search. All night, my mother cry, cry, cry. Morning time, they give up. The storm is over. Clear this morning and only a few big swells, a small wind to blow the flies away.

"High tide all the pools in the ocean in front of their place fill up like one bathtub. My mother is so tired, so dirty from all night hunting that she went out now in one big pool where always she like to shampoo her hair and take a bath. She is ready to step into the water when my father behind her shouts, 'Take care! Stay back! Shark!'

"She raise her hand to him to be quiet. She go on stepping into the water in the same pool. She sit there, her hair floating out all around her. The water in that pool is so clear. The sun shines on the sand and the wana and the shells on the bottom. The sun shines on the shape in the pool of one small shark.

" 'Auwe! Do not trust your aumakua so much!

137

Take care!' my father beg to her. 'What if one big shark, mother shark, stay hiding to come after you?'

"My mother shakes her head. She sits and waits for the small shark to come to her.

"The shark swims up. He grab at her breast in the water. 'Auwe!' My father jump in to save her, but no, she make a sign to him. He see, and he scare to see, the small shark drinking milk from her breast, a baby shark, a dark red mottled color like never he saw before in a shark, nursing on her.

"'It's him! Our baby! *Ehu* like his grand-mother. This is how I know him!' My mother cries, and now, ah, how happy she is. She smile and weep for joy."

Isaac paused and looked intently at Stanley. "Never you heard of such a thing, yuh?"

"Never," Stanley shuddered.

"Every day after that," Isaac went on, "My mother go in that same pool at high tide. Every day the small shark is there, waiting, and he comes to nurse on her. She sings and she talks to him. She strokes his head and back and belly. She loves him, that little red shark. He is her child. He doesn't eat the way shark eat, doesn't swallow the way shark swallow. He is like one human, only the shape of his body is shark."

Isaac cleared his throat and leaned to spit over

138

the side, watching the speed with which the canoe left the trace of spittle behind. "My brother, that one. You don't believe, Stanley? Ah, but you do. You do! I can tell! It happened. It can happen now like it happened then, forty—fifty years ago. Can happen now like it happened with the shark stone when my grandmother's grandmother's grandmother was a young girl. A human being can take the shape of a shark. A shark or a human being can change themselves into a stone. Mana. If a person has the power, he can still do such things. I could!"

"No!" Stanley protested. "Don't talk like that! Nobody should talk like that!" He put his hands to his ears.

"You don't want I should finish the story?" asked Isaac.

Stanley took his hands from his ears. He stared at the island coastline. He dared not stare at the surface of the ocean or at Isaac. "Please. I like to hear the rest."

Isaac shifted the steering paddle, heading them toward the distant point that was Wainalii. "Every day, my mother let the red shark nurse on her. By and by though, he get too big. Then every day my mother and father bring fish down to the tide pool to feed him. They get in the water and play, all three of them, because now my father recognize the

139

shark for his child, too, and he's no longer scared. He's happy, like her.

"One year pass and my mother is big in the belly with me. The red shark too big to get into the pool even at high tide. So, one day, sad like when any child grows up and leaves his homeplace, my mother and father go out to the reef and watch the red shark, their firstborn, my brother, swim off to make his own life in the open sea.

"When I am born, my grandmother wants me. That's Hawaiian custom, then and now. *Hanai*. My grandmother and me, we live in Wainalii, in a house same place my house is standing yet today. When I was a small boy growing up with her, every morning my grandmother took me down to the beach, the two of us. Sometimes the sharks come close inside the bay. My grandmother and me watch. We sometimes see one shark whose back looks reddish. 'Ah, there he is! That is your brother! That one, for sure!' my grandmother tell to me. 'He is waiting for you to be big enough to go out there where he lives. Swim out with him! Go visit him in your canoe. He take care for you out there. No scare any kind for you in the ocean or on it. The shark is your aumakua. You have a brother who is a shark!' "

Isaac's voice grew melancholy. "I was born the wrong time, Stanley. Better I live in the old days.

140

I feel that power, mana like the old ones knew, strong inside myself. Plenty times I come out here alone and I look for my brother. I learn the shark language to talk to him. So, last night, he and I could speak, and we did. Long time. I tell him about those haole men came to Wainalii yesterday. I tell him what they like to do to our old homeplace. I tell him, if that happen, if no place left for me to live how I like, I come out here and take for myself the same shape like my brother!"

"Don't say that! Don't think such things!" pleaded Stanley.

Isaac shrugged. "Only one place never can change from how it was in the old days, Stanley. That's my brother's homeplace, the sea. That's what him and me talked about, too, when you were sleeping."

Stanley looked fearfully out past the wake of the canoe.

"You do believe. You don't want to, but you do," said Isaac. "Funny. You do. And my own blood, Junior and Kimo, they no want to listen. Queenie, she no want for them to hear."

In silence, Isaac sailed on. In silence, Stanley sat thinking. A red shark who was Isaac's brother? No, that was too much! His imagination rebelled. Isaac was only telling him another story, like the old

141

legends that weren't really true. The only sounds were the rush of the water under the canoe, the strain of the sail in the wind, the slap and small rubbing noises of the lines, the occasional distraction of a jet flying overhead. Stanley's legs and back were cramped from crouching in the narrow canoe. His pajamas were soaked with salt spray. His eyes hurt from the glare of the sun on the water. His head ached from all the strange things Isaac had put in it.

"There," said Isaac. "Wainalii. Home, almost. Your father, he stay angry with me I think for take you out on the ocean without letting him know."

It was past three o'clock by the sun. Stanley looked from Isaac to the shoreline toward which they were sailing. He could see his father there, waiting. He could see his mother. Sheryl and Louise. Ba-chan . . . Everybody.

It was strange to see Wainalii from the reverse perspective of the sea. The sun glinted on the new tin roof of the school, on the new tins patching the roof of the store, on the people standing on the beach.

The canoe rode through the channel in the reef on a big swell.

"Like surfing, yuh?" said Isaac.

Stanley looked back at him.

"No scare," said Isaac. "I take all the blame, Stanley. I tell your father, your mother. No get after you. Me, I'm the one. I insist last night. I'm the

142

one knows better. I'm the one made you go. And I tell them. I'm the one had the right, now. They are your parents. But I *hanai* you Stanley, so now you have two fathers. Your own, natural father. And me!"

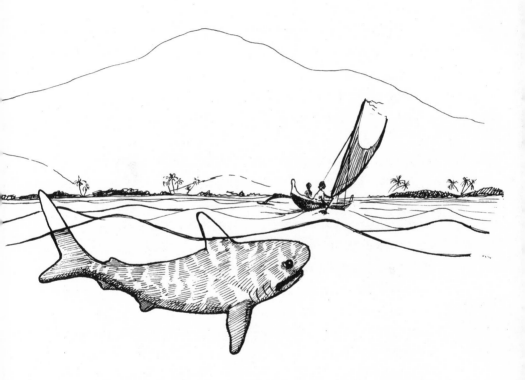

CHAPTER THIRTEEN

Stanley looked down at his pajamas. It had not occurred to him before how foolish he would feel coming home in the middle of the afternoon wearing nightclothes. He averted his eyes from shore, trying to postpone for as long as possible the necessity of having to face his father, and having to explain what he had done and why.

"Okay," said Isaac, without his usual confidence.

They both jumped out of the canoe into the shallow water. Stanley helped Isaac walk the canoe up onto the sand. "I'll help, Isaac," said Ichiro coming alongside Stanley. His voice was so stern it sounded unfamiliar. Stanley took a quick shamed sideways glance at his dad. Worse than he'd figured. He'd never seen him look like this before.

"I can do it alone okay, Ichiro," said Isaac.

"Go on, Stanley," said his father.

Stanley let his dad lift his end of the canoe and outrigger. He waded ashore, his pajama bottoms dragging in the water, his eyes carefully on his feet.

"You're going to get it! Oh, Stanley! You were bad!" His sister Sheryl came running up to him.

"Sheryl!" said their mother. "I told you to keep still!"

Stanley walked with the sand caking to his wet feet and his wet pajama bottoms. Without raising his eyes, speaking in a low voice he hoped only his mother would hear, he said, "I'm sorry. Mom, really I'm sorry. I didn't mean—"

"Stanley!" His father's stern tone stopped him. "You go up to the house. Take a shower. Get dry clothes on. And wait there for me."

Still limiting the world of his vision to the periphery of ground around his feet, Stanley walked up from the beach, conscious of people stepping back to let him pass by. He hurried through the palm grove, went into the house, got clean shorts and a T-shirt, went to the bathhouse and showered and changed. He rinsed out his pajamas in the washtubs outside and hung them on the line. Then he sat down on the bench under the milo tree and stared through the palm grove at the beach. His father and Isaac stood off to one side, the two of them, talking for a long time. It seemed to Stanley, straining to observe and attach meaning to each one's movements and gestures that the two did not part friends. Auwe! He bent double, hugging himself to stop the awful hunger cramps.

A few days later, Darwin Pahanui came home from Puna. He stopped at the store as soon as he changed out of his good clothes. Stanley was dusting soup cans that really did not need dusting, squatting lackadaisically with the feather duster in his hand and his mind wandering to some forbidden place with Isaac.

"Stanley! Come! Let's go down the beach!" urged Darwin.

Stanley shrugged. "Cannot."

"Well, tomorrow? Morning time? We go spear fish?"

"Cannot."

"Afternoon?"

Stanley shook his head and jabbed the feather duster across a row of pickle jars.

"Okay. You say when." Darwin looked puzzled.

"He can't leave our property for the rest of the summer. Unless he's with me." Stanley kept his face

146

expressionless, and his back to Darwin, as his father spoke up. "He's learning a lesson, Darwin. Fourteen —fifteen—no difference. You don't go off all night and all day someplace without letting your parents know."

Darwin gave Stanley a glance of sympathy and went off to find out from somebody else what terrible thing Stanley must have done.

Stanley's mother watched Darwin leave. The three of them were alone in the store. "I tell you! Every time I think about it. Stanley, how could you!"

Stanley tried not to close his ears but every day, all day, his mother kept after him with the same words.

"You're old enough to understand my condition! What might have happened with you giving me such worry—"

"Sueko, enough!" warned his father.

Stanley threw down the feather duster. He got up and ran out of the store, across the courtyard, up through the mango grove and back to the stone wall that was the property's boundary and his now, until school began. He wanted to cry, to yell, to run down to the beach, to do as he pleased. His skin ached for the feel of the ocean. He had not seen or talked to Isaac since they'd returned from the trip. Not being with Isaac, and being forbidden to see Isaac until September, that was hardest. Mondays and Thursdays he still got to go for mail and supplies with his father, but that he no longer enjoyed. His father never spoke, nor did he, all the way up the mountain and back.

Isaac did not come up to the store. He sent Queenie or Iwalani if he needed something. Every morning at dawn Stanley stood in the courtyard watching Isaac sail out in the canoe. He returned late, sometimes not until after dark. Queenie complained he never brought back fish, but Stanley knew it was not fish he went out for. "Not fair!" Stanley protested aloud to the barren hot slopes above the boundary wall. He picked up stones from the ground and began hurling them, as fast and hard as he could, letting the tears run down his face with no shame since there was no one around to see him. "Not fair! Mean! *Pilau!* I hate them!" he said with vehemence. Even as the words came out he was ashamed of them. He didn't really mean it. His father had not laid a hand on him—no licking, no paddling, no nothing but this awful confinement, this prohibition of the freedom to see and do all the things with the one person that, Stanley decided, he thought as much of as he did his parents. *Hanai.* That was how he felt toward Isaac. Like his son.

The days dragged by. Junior and Kimo came home from Honolulu. The Hilo relatives came weekends. They picnicked in the courtyard on the new

148

tables and benches Stanley helped his dad build. They all talked long and enthusiastically about Resco and the plans in the paper and how Stanley's family was going to be well off being here. "Although, I can't see why they picked this place!" said Aunt Hatsu. "It's much too hot over here!" When the men went fishing and crabbing at night, Stanley had to stay behind with the younger children. Not fair, he kept protesting inside. One week. Two weeks maybe. Not all summer long!

It did no good to sulk, to be angry, to argue, to come up to the boundary wall and throw rocks and think terrible thoughts. Impatiently, Stanley waited for the last long days of vacation to end.

Mr. Kainoa had the contract to drive the ones from Wainalii who went to high school. The trip, one way, was thirty-four miles. The first day when he got on the bus with Elizabeth Alapai and her brothers, and the Ii twins, and the older Pahanuis and Chings, Stanley felt like a prisoner released from jail. They rode up the mountain at half-past six. They got to school at seven forty-five.

Stanley stuck to the Wainalii gang when he could. He had a hard time finding his way around the high school. Four hundred students, smaller than the junior high he had attended in Chicago, but now four hundred students seemed to him an overwhelming number. It was four in the afternoon before the bus deposited him back in Wainalii. He had home-work every day, like he used to in Chicago. He had his work to do in the store before and after school. There was no time to go look for Isaac, although the prohibition on seeing him had ended. There was no time at home either to shift to hanging around with the bigger kids in Wainalii or to see his old friends who were still back in the eighth and ninth grades.

In October his mother went to Hilo to stay with Aunt Hatsu and Uncle Arthur until the new baby came. "A boy! A boy! You have a brother!" His father came rushing from a phone call as Stanley was leaving to catch the bus one morning. A brother? Stanley looked excited to please his dad, but a brother fourteen years younger didn't seem like a brother. Boy. Girl. The sex of the new baby made no real difference to him.

When he got home from school, his father had left for Hilo. The store was closed. Stanley didn't have to, but he took Sheryl and Louise down on the beach and played and swam with them until dusk. They were lonesome, with only Ba-chan and himself there.

That evening, for the first time since their trip in the canoe, Isaac came up. "Your momma gave birth? A boy? Ah, good! I'm happy for you folks." He put his hand on Stanley's shoulder. "Your papa,

he's still huhu with me, Stanley. It's going to take
him a while to forget. We be patient, though. You
wait. By and by the two of us we start going places
and doing things like before. You no forget while
you're waiting all the things I taught to you. You
work hard in school. You please your parents, whatever they ask of you. One month. Two month, I
figure. Then you and me go around together again.
Your father, he understand how I *hanai* you Stanley
—not real *hanai* like you coming to live in my house,
but *hanai* in the spirit, like how I share all I know
with you and pass certain things along to your care."
Isaac stood up from the bench under the milo tree
and stared out over the ocean. "Eh. What's that
coming?"

"One sail, looks like," said Stanley. They stood
watching. A few minutes and Yama Ching joined
them.

"Isaac," said Yama. "What kind sailboat is that
coming in?"

Isaac shook his head.

"Funny kind," said Stanley. "Sheryl! Louise!
You and Ba-chan come down the beach with us."
He walked, following Isaac and Yama, and guiding a
sister by each hand. Ba-chan, as excited as the children herself, hustled along scolding first at Sheryl
and then at Louise to be careful and mind their
brother, all of this in Japanese.

"Stay with Ba-chan, now!" Stanley told his sisters at the water's edge. He waded out with Isaac and Yama to watch the strange craft tack back and forth outside the reef. The afterglow of sunset was a red band on the horizon, the color staining the water and tinting the mountains. This, and sunrise, Stanley thought, were his two favorite times of day.

"How many years we don't see one yacht come to Wainalii?" said Yama as the sailboat found the channel and sailed through it.

Isaac spat. "Yacht! You take one more look with your eyes, Yama. No call that junks a yacht!"

"*Malolo*, Los Angeles." Stanley read off the name and the home port as the sailboat tacked first over around to the old pier and then back toward them. The beach filled with people like the day the helicopter had landed. "*Malolo*. Los Angeles!" yelled Junior.

"Los Angeles!" Mrs. Kainoa shouted up the beach to Emma Ching.

"He cross the ocean in that?" doubted Mateo Palabang. Isaac shook his head. "No can. Look how *kapulu* built. It wouldn't sail from here to Kawaihae!"

The *Malolo* veered closer. There was one man in the cockpit. "Anybody speak English?" he shouted.

"Sure!" Isaac called back.

Junior nudged Stanley. "Where does he think he is? Japan? Philippines?"

"I guess." Stanley laughed.

"Not Japan," said Darwin, who could be slow on a joke. "No palm trees in Japan, yuh Stanley?"

Isaac, Stanley, Yama, the Iis, Mateo, Junior and Darwin waded out waist deep to meet the vessel.

"How much you draw?" Isaac asked the man in the cockpit.

"Eighteen inches."

"Eighteen inches!" Yama whistled. "No wonder it looks how it looks!" He and Isaac grabbed the gunwhales and stubby bowsprit. Stanley helped them hold her and then turn her around so the bottom would not grate on the sand. The man aboard was a haole. His face was puffy with sunburn. His eyes were bloodshot, the skin pouched into bags underneath as if he had not had much sleep for a long time. He had red hair and a beard. First thing Stanley noticed was the rope tied around the man's waist and fastened at the other end to the base of the mast.

"Where am I at? Fiji? Canary Islands?" The man let the tiller swing free.

Stanley opened and shut his mouth. He looked at Isaac and then at Junior and Darwin. "Fiji!" whispered Junior. "Us cannibals. We gonna eat him. Only too skinny the kind!"

153

"Shut up you, Junior!" Isaac growled.

Stanley stared at the haole. Slack skin draped on his chest and belly. His lips were swollen blisters. "*Malolo*," said Stanley, embarrassed by Junior, "means flying fish?"

"Flying fish. That's right," said Isaac.

"*Malolo*. That there is a Haywaiian word," said the haole man. "A Haywaiian fellah in Los Angeles, he put me onto that name. You folks know some Haywaiian?"

"We are Hawaiian," said Isaac. "That's where you are. Wainalii. The Big Island. Hawaii. You got a few more thousand miles to go to Fiji. The Canary Islands, they weren't in this Pacific Ocean last time I saw a map."

"Hawaii?" The man sounded disappointed. "This is all the further I come in fifty-seven days?" He grabbed the tiller as if he still had to steer to get someplace. Then he let it go and laughed, a crazy kind of laugh. "I didn't know where I was going when I set out from Californy. I just figgered with all the islands there is strung out in this direction, if I kept going long enough I was bound to run into one of them." He looked beyond the men, up to where the women were standing around on the beach watching him. He ran his tongue over his swollen lips and crooked yellow teeth. His eyes were too

154

small for the size of his face, Stanley decided, studying him.

"Vye—nah—what did you say?"

Isaac repeated the name. "It's not on the big chart of the islands. Only on the chart of this coast. You have that aboard?"

The man tried to stand up. He was too weak. He sank into the cockpit. "Charts? I saw some in L.A., but I don't read that good. Couldn't tell what I was looking at on them unless they had some made with pictures so you can tell, like in comic books." He grinned. "Out on that ocean you don't know where you're at oncet you get out of sight of the shore. So what good is a map?"

"You got an anchor?" Isaac asked. "Hard on us trying to hold this boat too long."

"Somewheres. I don't remember. Maybe it got washed overboard. Lots of stuff did. I hit bad weather two days out of L.A. My rudder broke five days out. I kept the line from the mainsail wound around the tiller handle because the cleat come off the second week. I sort of had to go where the wind took me. Then the mast went thirty days out. I rigged the sail how you see. So, I ain't had the occasion to look for my anchor or to even think about one." He scratched his beard. He didn't look into the cabin where an anchor might be. He looked up

155

the beach at the women. "Shucks," he said wistfully. "No grass skirts."

"You give us a line, and we make one rock anchor, or tie you to swing between coral heads," Isaac offered.

The haole appeared not to be listening. "I ain't seen nobody for so long," he said. "I ain't talked. All I done is to steer, and try not to doze off to miss nothing, and try not to eat much so my provisions would hold out. I'd of went crazy without I had my rifle. And plenty of shells. So I could keep my mind right shooting at sharks." He patted a plastic-wrapped bundle wedged under his feet in the cockpit. "On the way acrost, I bet I shot ten sharks. Off'n here this morning, I took aim at a big one I seen."

Stanley looked at Isaac.

"Around here," said Isaac, "we let the sharks have their part of the ocean when they want. Don't you go shooting at any!"

"Yeah?" The haole glanced down at his rifle. His eyes fixed on the sheath knife stuck in the belt of his jeans. "I almost forgot. I didn't mark off for today." He pulled the knife free and leaned forward, adding a gouge to the series of marks in the framing around the cabin door. "That there's my calendar," he said proudly. "That's how I kept track of the days going by. At sea, they're all alike, one

156

day after another. Your head gets full of funny no-
tions. It helps, having sharks to shoot at and something like them marks to count." He started counting
aloud, looked confused, stopped, and sighed. "Fifty-
six? Fifty-seven? I forget." He waited with a childish expectant expression while the men, in unison,
began counting the marks on the door frame.

"Fifty-six!" Stanley called out.

"Fifty-six!" Isaac confirmed.

The man frowned. "What is today? Saturday?
Tuesday? All I know is it's almost dark. One more
day to notch off. And I'm in Hawaiyah. No grass
skirts!" He giggled.

Moses Ii gave him the date. "Wednesday?" the
man repeated. The month, or the date of the month
didn't interest him. Stanley repeated the date. "I
don't care," he said. "I ain't going no place else. I
been, these fifty-six days! It's Wednesday? I'm going
to stay put here. My name's Tompkins. Archer
Tompkins. I can find me a job here as quick as the
next place, I bet you. Pull me up on the beach, you
guys!"

They pushed to Isaac's signal. With the next
surge, they maneuvered the *Malolo* inshore so that
her bottom rested solidly on the sand.

"Wow!" Stanley stretched out his arms.

"Strains the muscles, to hold her so long, yuh?"
said Isaac.

Yama rubbed his arms too. "You're right, Isaac!" he grinned. "She's no yacht!"

The *Malolo* could not have been less like the sleek flying fish for which she was named. She was twenty-five feet long with an eight-foot beam. The cabin was plywood with square window-glass portholes. The hull was a surplus rubber life raft with a plywood superstructure. The deck was covered with strips of tar paper roofing. The rigging was baling wire and clothesline. A board had been nailed across the bottom of the cabin door in an attempt at a storm hatch. Inside, the single bunk was piled with dirty wet blankets.

A collection of paraffined cans of food, plastic sacks of rifle shells, comic books, cooking pots, and cans of Sterno floated on the cabin floor.

"Fifty-six days. I was sure this was Fiji!" Archer Tompkins fumbled to untie the line around his waist. Failing, he took the sheath knife and cut the rope. "There!" he said, "I won't worry I might get washed overboard and et by them sharks anymore!" He stood up. His legs buckled. "Everything's moving around!"

Isaac reached over, picked the man up, and carried him like a baby from the boat to the shade at the edge of the palm grove. Archer Tompkins sat there, his fingers clutching the sand in grasping incredulous handfuls. "I want my rifle! Bring me my rifle!" he demanded. Stanley brought the plastic-wrapped rifle from the cockpit. Archer Tompkins snatched it, cradled it in his lap, and grinned. "Hawaiyah? I tell you what. I'll set up a camp on the beach here. You folks can bring me coconuts and fish and bananas and stuff. Like I seen in the movies," said Archer Tompkins. He pointed a curious finger at Stanley. "Boy. You're the only Jap this place, you and your folks?" His nod included Ba-chan and the two little girls.

"Japanese," said Isaac swiftly, with a scowl. "And so what if they are? No big thing who you are around here!"

"I'm hungry," said Archer Tompkins, leaning his back against a palm trunk. Stanley looked at him with instant dislike. Isaac shook his head and sighed.

"These haoles!" grumbled Yama Ching.

CHAPTER FOURTEEN

Next day after school when Stanley took his sisters down to the beach, Mateo was presenting the haole with a half-sack of rice and a package of dried fish. "You don't know anybody who'd give me a carton of cigarettes, do you, boy?" Archer Tompkins asked Stanley. He accepted Mateo's gifts without a thank you.

Stanley shrugged. Archer Tompkins sat on an old car seat Yama had brought him. He smelled of beer and sweat. He was belching and swatting flies and ordering Junior and Kimo and Darwin what to do.

"You!" he commanded Stanley. "You help them other boys pry loose my bunk from the boat.

Mateo, you take that there piece of sail. You can rig me a windbreak between the trees. You! Darwin? Go get some fellas to help and bring me a picnic table outen that park. Nobody got a extry lantern home so I can see around my camp at night? Kimo. That's your name, Kimo? Helluva name for a kid. Kimo, you bring some rock off that stone wall. We'll build me a fireplace."

Until dark, the boys and Mateo helped Archer Tompkins while Sheryl and Louise climbed off and on *Malolo* and looked at Archer's comic books.

"He's a stranger. He came to our place. We have to help him how we can," Junior said when Stanley questioned why they should all work so for the haole man.

It annoyed Stanley how Archer Tompkins sat on the car seat bossing them and doing nothing himself.

"He's weak, that's why," said Darwin.

"And he's haole," said Kimo. "Haoles, they like to boss."

Every morning now at dawn Stanley stood in the courtyard listening to Archer Tompkins shoot at the doves, at the mynah birds, at the stray mongoose down to sniff the rubbish barrel in the park. "No good bugger, that one!" predicted Isaac waiting with Stanley for the school bus. "He better take care where he shoots with that gun!"

161

Stanley's dad came home from Hilo. His mother and the new baby would stay with Aunt Hatsu for the first month.

One Saturday afternoon Stanley went down to the beach by himself to go for a swim. There was a branding luau up at the ranch. Everybody, almost, in Wainalii had gone. Stanley wished his father would let him accept Isaac's invitation to go with him, but he didn't get up the courage to ask. Out in the canoe. Up to the ranch. His father wasn't ready to let him be with Isaac too much yet, Stanley knew.

At midafternoon the store was quiet. His dad was busy with some book work for the post office. The two girls were taking naps. Ba-chan was up in the house dozing, with the Japanese radio program turned on full volume.

"Go!" his dad urged. "Take off and enjoy a swim. Maybe take your spear and bring back a *tako* for me to take to Aunt Hatsu tomorrow when I go in."

Stanley avoided Archer's camp, walking around through the palm grove to the far side near the pier. Archer Tompkins was sitting on his car seat shooting at a mongoose who lived in the base of the stone wall. He had spent money on nothing else, but he was up with cash to buy shells at the store every couple days.

"Excuse, please," Stanley said to Isaac's kaku as

he swam out closer than usual to the shadows of the pier. He fancied the kaku would recognize him as it recognized Isaac. Stanley had no fear about swimming alone in or outside the bay. He swam to the shore side of the reef, spear ready, hunting the holes where an octopus might live. A small mound of gravel or sand piled in telltale fashion beside a hole. That was the sign. Twice, Stanley found places he thought were like the ones Isaac had showed him.

In each promising-looking place, Stanley jabbed his spear. Nothing. Then out in the open he saw what looked like a moving branched piece of pink coral. It changed color as he watched it. It changed texture, from a smooth to a rough goosefleshed surface like the grainy texture of a coral. *"Tako!"* Stanley recognized. There was the eye and a beak mouth in the camouflage. He jabbed with his spear. The octopus sent out a cloud of reddish-brown fluid, discoloring the water, hiding itself and the spear point in a murk that darkened in color as it dispersed. Stanley held the spear steady, impaled against the bottom so the octopus could not writhe off. When he saw it was secure, he lifted the spear and swam to a shallow spot where the reef emerged to a brown weed-drenched islet. He slid onto it and sat there, turning the creature's body inside out with the deft motion Isaac had taught him. That way the beak mouth could not bite.

163

The tentacles writhed around the spear and up around his hands and arms. It was a queer sensation, the suction cups of the tentacles gripping his skin. Stanley laughed, out here on the reef all by himself. If anybody had told him, last year in Chicago, that he'd enjoy playing with an octopus, and look forward to eating it, he'd not have believed him. He strung the octopus on the line he carried attached to a plastic bleach jug float. He towed it behind him, taking his time to look around at the reef before beginning the swim in.

Close to the channel, in water fifteen feet deep, Stanley saw an enormous form in the water ahead of him. It was a manta ray of such size that his first impulse was to backwater, turn, and swim quickly away. He had seen small rays on trips outside the reef with Isaac. This one–Stanley hesitated. It was shaped like a delta-wing jet. The flaps moved through the water with a slow powerful beat in the same graceful fashion as an eagle or hawk might fly through the ocean of air that pressed down on this ocean of water. Ten feet long? Fifteen feet from wing tip to wint tip? The tail alone was longer than he was tall. The eyes were the size of dishpans.

Stanley took a deep breath, jackknifed, and dived to the bottom. He hung onto a coral head. The ray circled above him. It swerved, swooped down. Isaac had said the manta ray could use the sharp razors on its tail only if it were anchored in sandy bottom, but he was not at all eager to put the information to a test. The ray's eyes followed his every movement, as curious about him as he was about it. It swam closer. Stanley surfaced. The ray followed him up.

Stanley slapped the surface of the water with the flat of his hand. He opened his mouth and shouted underwater. At each noise, the creature hesitated, but only long enough to let Stanley get a more comfortable distance away. It was a dozen strokes behind and to one side of him. Stanley tried to keep it in view. He pulled the diving knife from his belt. It felt puny but he held onto it anyway, swimming as hard and fast as he could toward shore. Halfway in, Stanley sensed a strange motion passing close to him through the water. A queer tearing vibration, and something passing just outside his mask's range. Something pinged the surface close to his shoulder. Stanley lifted his head out of the water. On the beach stood Archer Tompkins with his rifle, his finger squeezing the trigger, the barrel aimed directly at him.

"Hey! No! Stop!" yelled Stanley. He dove down hugging the bottom, swimming underwater until his lungs felt as if they had to have air.

Ping! Ping! Ping! The shells hit the water around him. The manta ray dropped behind, turned, and swam out. Stanley gulped a deep breath, dove, and swam underwater another long stretch. *Ping! Ping! Ping!* He swam in a fast detour toward the pier. In the shallows, he crouched behind the protection of a shoreside piling. Archer Tompkins was shooting now at a ripple of wind across the middle of the bay.

Stanley walked cautiously from behind the piling, up along the beach. In the pass, the twin flaps of the giant ray dipped above the surface. Archer aimed and shot and missed. Then he swerved and took aim at the long dark shadow of Isaac's kaku cruising out from the pier in answer to signals that sounded confusingly like Isaac's paddle smacking the water.

Stanley rushed across the sand and tackled Archer Tompkins. The rifle spun from Archer's hands. Stanley ran fast to get out of reach of Archer's angry grasp.

"I would of got him!" Archer picked up his rifle and shook the sand off it. "I hate sharks. I hate 'em! Them two follering you in. I almost got them. That big one under the pier. I'm gonna kill him one of these days like I would have just now!" Archer raised his rifle, turned his back on Stanley, and aimed again toward the pier. "You trip me again and I'll shoot you!" he threatened. His finger curled on the trigger. "Damn," he screamed. The rifle was empty. Stanley sprinted to the piling. The kaku was safely back in the shadows. He retrieved his octopus, and raced home.

"Eh! What's all the shooting down there?" his dad wanted to know. He came out from the store with his reading glasses pushed down on his nose, looking at Stanley over the top of the black plastic frames.

"Archer Tompkins. Shooting at Isaac's kaku," said Stanley. He was so out of breath, he flopped on the steps.

"Sure nice *tako*. No wonder you're worn out catching him!" his dad admired. He frowned as the shots resumed from the beach. "Archer Tompkins better take care. He shoot Isaac's kaku, Isaac will shoot him!"

CHAPTER FIFTEEN

"Free day for you Stanley," said his father the next morning. "I get your mother and the baby from Hilo today. Ba-chan can look after the girls. We close the store. I trust you, Stanley. You learned your lesson. You know where to go and where not to. Anyplace you like is okay with me, only not out with Isaac in his canoe!"

The older friends Stanley hung around with at school were still up at the ranch today helping brand. He hunted up Junior and Kimo and Darwin. It was like last year, being out with them. The sea was a flat deep blue. The water was clear. The air was hot from the November sun.

"Hey. You growing more tall, Stanley!" noticed

Darwin. "You get more tall than Kimo since June."

"I guess." Stanley tried not to look too pleased that his friends had noticed.

"You shave every day now!"

"Must be something, to go to the high school, yuh?" said Junior.

"It's okay," said Stanley. The questions, and the way his three friends regarded him as older and more experienced made him aware how changed he was.

The four of them spent the long hot Sunday roaming where fancy took them and, because of his seniority, to wherever Stanley wanted most to go. They walked up and down past Archer's campsite. They swam out into the bay. They hiked to the lighthouse point, where they sat and threw stones into the clear water. They chased crabs over the jumble of lava boulders. They sat and traded news.

"More better I stayed home from Puna the summer," anguished Darwin. "All my life I never see one helicopter yet. And to think I missed it. Auwe!"

"My father, he's huhu what they trying to do, those men who came in the helicopter and all the rest in the government," said Junior. "He get letter already, offer us land exchange. They say, by and by pretty soon they bring paper for us to sign. Only him, he say he no sign."

"Strong, your father," Darwin admired. "Mine,

he sign the paper already and sent 'em back. He no like sign, but he say no sense argue because no matter what, the government they going do what they want."

Until it was dusk, the boys spearfished. They had a washtub floated in an inner tube and the four of them filled it with fish. "Archer Tompkins is sick today I think," said Junior. "He don't shoot his rifle one time!"

"He's out of shells," guessed Stanley. "Lucky the store is closed today. Give us some peace."

Junior was helping Stanley carry his share of the fish home when his father drove into the courtyard.

"Nice baby," said Junior politely, admiring the bundle of blankets and wrinkled red face, the long shock of black hair and screwed-up features that were Stanley's new brother.

Stanley had forgotten how strange a new baby was—the eyes that didn't quite focus, the wobbly head that had to be carefully held, the incredibly tiny hands and feet, the determined way they could cry. He looked at his new brother and said to himself, my brother. This is really my brother. He felt a rush of pride and affection and reached out impulsively to put a finger into the tiny clutching fist. "Ahhhhh! Jason! You smile at me!" Stanley grinned.

As he had suspected, once his mother and his baby brother were home, the household no longer ran

170

by the sun, or by the store schedule, or by the bus and bell for school. Nights, everyone woke up when Jason Hideo did. Daytimes, either his mother or Ba-chan was always washing diapers or holding the baby or feeding him. Louise ran around being naughty because none of them paid much attention to her anymore. She was lonely daytimes since Sheryl had started school.

Stanley's father was extra busy, preparing for the construction men the newspaper report had said would be moved into Wainalii by the Resco resort project before the first of the year. Ichiro had gotten a loan from the bank to build two motel units up back of the courtyard near the house. He rented a portable concrete mixer. He hired Archer Tompkins, who turned out to be as expert a construction worker as he claimed.

Every day when Stanley came home from school he could see the progress on the units. Foundations poured. Concrete block walls taking shape. They had only three more courses of blocks to lay to reach the roof line when Stanley left for school one morning. At four o'clock that afternoon, his dad and Archer Tompkins had temporarily abandoned their work, and with the rest of the family were standing in the driveway of the store watching.

Blocking the usual turnoff of the school bus onto the coral road was a truck with a mammoth bulldozer on its gooseneck trailer. It was stuck, blocking both the way into the palm grove and the road on to the dead end of the pier. "Whatsa mattah him, the stupid!" said Mr. Kainoa. "He's too wide and heavy to turn that way!" He parked the bus along the roadside. Stanley hurried out with the rest to see what was happening.

"They never make it! They can't back in or out of there!" Yama Ching was predicting.

Moses Ii stood beside him, offering his opinion. "They ought to unhook the cab from the trailer. Get one more truck down. Winch the stuck one out."

Old Ah Fook, on his way home from his afternoon walk, stood braced on his guava stick and his tottery legs, amazed to find such an obstacle in his way. "No use for say anything to these Honolulu guys," grumbled Yama to Mr. Kainoa. "I told them. Don't take the gooseneck to unload in there. Start the other side. From the pier. Then, no trouble." He made a face. "They're not the kind to listen."

The driver, a Portuguese with a blue hard hat on his head, scowled at Yama. "Ahhhhhh," he contradicted. "Nobody gives advice until I get stuck. I ask two guys. Okay come this way? All they say is, oh, they don't know!"

"Cool it," said the helper in the truck. "We're stuck, we're stuck. No good argue about why."

Stanley saw Isaac at the far side of the crowd. He

172

started to join him and then, abashed, swerved to stand beside his father. "They bring one bulldozer to start already! Fast, yuh?" said his father, pleased.

Nobody else looked happy.

"I'm gonna call Kaumanua," said Mr. Kainoa. "What else we sent him to the legislature for? These guys come down for move our house, and he nor nobody let us know ahead of time!"

"We sign only one week ago. Too soon, they start this. Nobody ever move so fast before!" complained Yama.

"Isaac, you sign yet?" asked Moses Ii.

"Never," said Isaac. "I tell you, all of you when you signed last week. Hold off. But no. You ask no questions. You don't call up nobody. Now, with your name on the paper, you have to go where and when this Resco say."

"Aaaaaaah! I call that Kaumanua tomorrow morning. Collect!" Moses Ii spit into the salt-caked earth and ground the spittle with his slipper sole.

All the while they were complaining, the two men in the truck were trying to get out. The motor whined and strained. The wheels spun and dug deeper with each try. Ah Fook stood watching, mouth ajar. To his ancient eyes, Stanley imagined, the bulldozer squatting on the trailer must look like a strange yellow dragon with its monstrous flat teeth of treads and great powerful blade.

"The equipment down here and nobody tell us make ready for move house. Nobody give us our new lot number the other side yet. You men. You don't speak up on this!" said Mrs. Kainoa. "You wait. Next election I tell off that Kaumanua when he comes around shake hands and ask for my vote!"

"You think anybody cares if a little guy don't like what a big guy does to you?" asked Archer Tompkins. "The way I see it, you might as well make the best of it. If an outfit like Resco is coming in, you're better off to go along with them. Now me. I'm a mind to call up and ask for a job with them. I ain't proud. I hear they promised all of us down here one. A dollar's a dollar. Where I earn it don't make any difference to me. I like to drink and I like to shoot. Takes cash money. More'n I got left from fitting out from the trip. More'n I can make working oncet in a while for you, Ichiro. Hey you guys!" He stepped up to the cab. Both doors were open. The driver hung half out on his side trying to see where his back wheels were going. His sweat-soaked shirt was a second skin on his back. Sweat gleamed on his face. Streaks of grease marked his forehead and cheeks and neck. His helper ran back and forth alongside the cab shouting signals.

"Now if I was you," Archer began. The two men ignored him.

"Don't yell when your back wheels slide off into

174

the salt muck like they're going to if you keep on."

"He's right!" agreed Yama.

Archer stood beside Moses Ii.

"There!" said Isaac.

"Auwe!" exclaimed Stanley. The big double wheels spun up out of the sand, hovered, and then slid off into the salt ooze of the pond.

"They don't move nobody's house today!" grinned Mateo.

"Can they get the truck out?" asked Stanley.

"Tomorrow," his dad assumed. "They back the bulldozer off the trailer. Mud, nothing, no matter to one big machine like that. They can use the bulldozer to pull the truck out, if they hook a cable on."

The two men in the truck cab got out and stood smoking cigarettes.

"The way them two is going at it, they ain't gonna get unstuck tomorrow nor the day after," said Archer. "I run one of them big D-9's one time in Texas. I know."

Archer sounded right. People began to leave to go about their fishing, or their chores, or to go lie down under the trees and enjoy a nap. Stanley went up to the store to work. Isaac disappeared into his house. Ah Fook was one of the last to leave. Finally he too started off, but the afternoon excitement confused him so that instead of walking on home, he began his regular afternoon pilgrimage a second time.

The next morning the truck and the gooseneck were still there. The bulldozer squatted impotently on the trailer bed. The two workmen spent the night with Mateo. Archer was up at six to start work on the units, which Ichiro was impatient to finish. "We could have rented them out last night already!" he said. "I spoke to the foreman. A few days more. When he's ready to come down here, we'll have those places finished enough to move in a bed. They can use our bathhouse. No matter if the plumbing fixtures didn't come yet."

By late afternoon, the bulldozer had been backed off the trailer at the expense of three tall coconut palms. They lay across the village path, their slender trunks prone. The splintered torn mass of roots wrenched from the ground left a broad shallow crater swarming with processions of ants.

Isaac was standing alone, staring at the bulldozer when Stanley went down.

"That truck, it doesn't want to come out from the pond, Stanley," said Isaac in a queer way. "That bulldozer, it doesn't want to work down here."

"Ah, Isaac!" Stanley stared at him. This was too much—like Isaac claiming a red shark as a brother. A truck that had volition? That did not want to be moved and therefore would not move? A bulldozer that had will, and willed not to work in a certain place? It made him uneasy to have Isaac talk about machines,

176

big impersonal man-made machines in such a way. Stones, maybe. Sharks, who knew? But—bulldozers. Stanley shook his head.

The following day, a foreman named Ohta came down in a jeep to take charge. The bulldozer, willing or not, was backed off the trailer. In its first charge through the palm grove, it ate out ten trees and broke a tread.

When Stanley got off the bus, the difference hurt his eyes. He could see things in the village he'd never noticed before—like junk that had been camouflaged by shadows and tree trunks.

Isaac was there watching the foreman and the two men try to fix the bulldozer tread. "They're not going to take more trees out?" said Stanley, aghast at how different Wainalii appeared.

The foreman and the two men paid no attention to him.

"No more," said Isaac with a queer smile. "No more trees wants to go. That bulldozer he get sore teeth from eating all those coconut trees. Tomorrow, I don't think he try to eat any more."

"Don't say that!" said the Portuguese driver. He tried to sound like he was joking, but his eyes were afraid and uneasy looking. "If the machine don't work, I don't work. If I don't work, I don't get paid."

The next day, which was Saturday, the men went to Hilo for the weekend. Monday afternoon, when

177

the bus brought him home, Stanley wanted to stay down and watch the five extra men replace the tread on the bulldozer, but he had to help his dad. By dusk they had put the roof on the new units. The workmen rented them that night. Part of the arrangement was for Stanley's mother to furnish them three meals a day. Stanley had to help her serve. The men ate at the new tables in the courtyard.

That night, Stanley was too tired to do his homework, and his mother was too busy to get after him. In the morning, he helped serve breakfast to the men at six. He had to run to catch the bus for school.

Tuesday another truck arrived, and Mateo announced, "The trailer he decide he like to move out from the pond."

Wednesday Stanley came home to the ugly sound of the bulldozer leveling palm trees. His eyes flinched from the spectacle of a naked village. Only a sorry fringe of palms was left around Isaac's house.

They can't! He kept telling himself. They can't! They wouldn't. It hurt to look. It hurt to listen to the dying trees that had shaded Wainalii since before Isaac was born.

Stanley dragged his feet up the steep driveway of the store. He stood disconsolately in the courtyard looking at the new view. The weathered houses stood out in the open sun. The junk was unobscured by patterns of shade. The beach was an ordinary beach with its line of canoes and old oil barrels and a tide mark of debris.

Maui still floated blue and lofty on the horizon. The surf broke in white curds against the reef. The sun glistened on the obelisk of the lighthouse. The kiawes were a dense, thorny screen around the hidden clearing. The park and the stone boundary wall were intact. Everything else was changed. A few of the women waded lackadaisically out in the bay. Several children played in the water. Stanley shielded his eyes with his hand, straining to see offshore from Archer Tompkins' camp a trace of moving shapes cutting the bay surface. Archer was standing at the water's edge, rifle poised.

"Shark! Shark! Isaac! *Kokua*! Come! Quick!"

The crack of Archer's rifle was an exclamation point to Emma Ching's scream.

Stanley raced to the beach. Isaac ran down from his verandah. "Archer! You! Tompkins! No shoot at them!" Isaac rushed at Archer, knocked the rifle to the sand. Archer went reeling from the blow of his huge fist. Isaac picked up the rifle, opened it, removed the shells, and hurled the unused shells into the water. "Emma!" he ordered. "You put this away in your house for Mr. Tompkins. He's not going to use it now. I don't want him shooting at me while I swim my friends out of the bay." Isaac turned to Stanley. "This is the season they lose their head sometimes and all get lost in here. I have to show them the way, how to go out. Iwalani! Go get my mask, fins, the bag—you know what one."

Stanley hesitated. "I can go with you, Isaac?"

Isaac gave him a long keen appraisal. "No scare?"

"No scare for me, with you, anywhere on the ocean!" said Stanley. He turned to run home for his own mask and fins. "You tell your father you're going!" said Isaac.

Stanley nodded. He hurried through the devastated village, leaping over the fallen palm trunks and jumping the craters left by their uprooting. He ran past the trucks and the bulldozer and the foreman and the crew, across the road, up the drive, and into the house. He changed to swim shorts, picked up his mask and fins. "I'm going with Isaac. Swimming out in the bay. Not for long!" he called to his dad as he paused on the verandah of the store.

Mr. Sasaki came out, his glasses on his nose, a pen in his hand. "Those plumbing fixtures, they didn't come on today's barge," he said absentmindedly. "Oh. Swimming?" He frowned. "I heard somebody yell shark from the beach a while ago?"

"Only a few of them," said Stanley. He started down.

"Stanley!"

He paused, dreading to look back for fear of what his father might be realizing.

"Archer never came back from lunch to work this afternoon. I still could use him, tell him. I like him to come up work a few hours. And you too."

"Okay. In a while," Stanley assured, and hurried back to the beach.

CHAPTER SIXTEEN

Emma Ching had not exaggerated.

"Plenty shark!" said Stanley looking out at the bay. He sat down beside Isaac to put on his mask and fins.

"You're crazy! You'll get et!" said Archer Tompkins. "Stanley, your pa and ma don't mind for you to go out there?"

"You tell them, Stanley?" said Isaac.

Stanley nodded. "My father said he like for you to come up and work for him the rest of this afternoon, Archer."

Archer rubbed his sore mouth and gave Isaac a mean look. "I'll go up." He shook his head. "I could take care of all them shark for you fast!" He raised an imaginary rifle barrel and squinted, cocking his finger. "One! Two! Three! I'd get every one 'a 'em!"

"Shut up you!" growled Isaac.

Archer made a face. "I was only fooling! Honest!" He stepped back. "I oughta be good and mad at you for hauling off and hitting me like that, and for taking my rifle, and for throwing them good shells away. If you wasn't bigger than me—"

"Okay," said Isaac, ignoring Archer Tompkins. "Stanley, us go." He looked out over the bay with the oblique gaze he had used to gauge the numbers and location of the fish the day they'd gone up the coast thrownetting. "Plenty of them," he said. Then, in a low voice only Stanley could hear, "I don't think he came in here today. But maybe he's outside. We'll see." Isaac tied the cotton bag to the waistband of his shorts. Easily as if he were some great fish returning to an element where he belonged, he slipped full length into the water. Stanley followed him.

"They'll get et!" he heard Archer Tompkins say. From a distance, he heard his father running toward the beach, calling his name. Stanley kept his head down, his face in the water, his fins kicking him along at a steady pace.

The water was milky today, and stray cold currents circulated in the warm shallow water of the bay. Fifty feet offshore, the long gray shark shapes surrounded the two of them. Isaac never changed his powerful slow crawl. He never once raised his head to look behind at the naked village or the people on the beach.

"Come! *Hele mai!*" he said softly, his eyes on the circling sharks. "*Hele mai!*" he urged as if he were calling hunting dogs to follow him.

Stanley swam warily, as close to Isaac as he could. He watched the sharks through his mask. His heart was pounding so that the noise of it seemed a din in his ears. Surely Isaac would hear and know he was a little afraid.

Isaac swam faster until he had maneuvered ahead of the lead shark. Then, he swung out of the circle pattern they had set for themselves. Instead of swimming from the reef across to the pier as they had been doing, he and Stanley led them through the pass in the reef. Isaac smacked the water with his hand. "Come!" he called to the sharks. He motioned to Stanley to swim in a small circle, waiting for the right instant in the surge of surf breaking at the reef. Then, with the outrace of water, the two of them went on out through the channel. The sharks followed. Isaac raised his head and looked back at them. "Good. *Maikai!*"

They led the sharks past the coral shelves and valleys of the outer reef, over the underwater arches

184

and tunnels left by drowned ancient lava flows, on a course out into the deep open sea. Far below them schools of fish fed and flowed along the bottom. Good eating fish there below in easy range, but of interest neither to the sharks nor to them today.

A sea turtle passed close enough so Stanley could have reached out and poked its huge oval shell. The second shark in the procession swam up and circled beneath the turtle. He snapped at it, and missed. Isaac yelled in an angry warning voice below the surface of the water. He slapped the water with the flat of his hand, making a big noise. He feinted with his spear, prodding the shark back into his place. "Some of you are so stupid!" he said.

For an hour, Isaac and Stanley swam the sharks out until, when Stanley raised his head to look back, the buildings of the village were miniatures in the distance. He was too far out to be able to see any figures on the shore. The cloud-shrouded high mountains of the island's interior loomed an impressive size against the sky. In the late-afternoon light, every deep gulch and valley, every dry stream bed, the patches of forest, and the dark scars of old lava flows on their upper flanks stood out in detail.

"Okay. Go on now," Isaac admonished the sharks. "Find someplace else. But don't you go back in the bay! You scare the Wainalii people. You remember, you stupid one," he spoke to the second of the sharks, the one who had snapped at the turtle. "You. Stay out from that bay!"

Isaac turned over, floating on his back, but keeping his arms and legs moving, resting while five of the sharks kept swimming away.

"Isaac. Take care!" warned Stanley.

The sixth shark, the biggest, broke away and swam in a detour around Isaac, his black fin cutting a closer and closer circle in the water.

Isaac turned over. Stanley watched through his mask. A big one, an old one this shark—but it was not red. Isaac reached out and gave the shark's side a prod with his spear. "Eh! Come over, you poor thing, you! I help you. I clean you up!"

The shark circled away at the spear's prod. Isaac swam after it, talking to it the whole while as if surely the shark could hear and understand, using the same words he would use to make friends with a stray dog. Stanley followed, watching with awe.

In a while, the shark let Isaac come close so he could climb up on the great rough back. "You poor thing, you! The coral all grown in your eyes, and everywhere, and all limu! How could you see me to know who I was?" Isaac lay along the length of the shark, crooning, talking, reassuring. He undid the

186

cotton bag from his waist and took out a chisel and a screwdriver, held the tools in his teeth while he tied the bag to his waist again and handed his spear to Stanley to hold. Chipping, scraping, prying, with his tools and his two powerful hands, Isaac cleaned the coral and moss from the shark's back. He carefully cleaned the head and the small eyes. He dived under and cleaned off the belly. He kept well out of the way of the ugly mouth. "It might forget, like one dog forgets, and snap at me. Instinct. Some not too smart you know!" he told Stanley.

The cleaning took a long time. Isaac's hands, his body, his tools, stank of shark. His skin had scrape marks from the scaly skin. When he slipped off the shark's back to swim free, it followed him—a piece of two-by-twelve floated on the surface. Stanley swam quickly out of the way as the shark turned over and came up from beneath to snap at the timber.

"Mind!" warned Isaac, his eyes and his spear wary.

Three times the shark turned and came up and tried to swallow the two-by-twelve. "It's as long as he is!" said Stanley.

"Enough. Enough!" said Isaac. "Hsssssss-ahhhhh!" He opened his mouth and shouted under the water. "Go. Go on now. You all fixed up. You hungry. Only, not for that. And not for me!" Isaac brandished his spear. He slapped the water and kept moving away from the big shark. Hssss-ahhh! Go!" he yelled. He and Stanley watched, keeping their eyes on the gray shape until it swam off and away.

The wind was rising. The tide was turned. "The tide help us now. And we catch one current I know to take us in. You tired, Stanley?" asked Isaac.

"Only cold." Stanley's fingertips were pinched into deep white grooves. They felt numb. His skin was gooseflesh.

"Swim fast a little bit. We warm you up," said Isaac. "Okay? Better now? No hurry. We go the speed best for you."

Looking up, for a few strokes while he rested on his back, Stanley saw a freighter heading for Maui. A school of porpoise dived around them. "Good fun, yuh?" Isaac called. He and Stanley dived and played among them until the school went on.

Outside the reef, over a fish hole that often gave him a dinner, Isaac speared an ulua. Stanley tried for a smaller fish, and missed. They came in across the bay, side by side, as if they swam in from an ordinary afternoon's spearing. "Too good, you, Stanley!" said Isaac before they reached shore.

Stanley was dismayed, seeing his father standing waiting for them, with everyone else on the beach. He looked up to where his mother stood in the drive-

188

way watching the beach, with the baby on her shoulder.

"Your momma, she didn't like that you went with Isaac. But I told her, you said to me where you were going. I had my mind on the order didn't come on the Hilo barge, you know that? Until you left, I didn't think about what you were going to do!" Ichiro grabbed Stanley's arm and squeezed it in a relieved, affectionate embrace.

"Tell her! Tell Emma give me back my rifle now, Isaac!" said Archer Tompkins. He looked and sounded childish. His swollen mouth was puffed up in a pout. No use to hate him, thought Stanley. He's how he is because he isn't very smart. "I'm sorry to worry Momma," said Stanley to his father.

"Pahanui was ready to go out for you in his canoe with Yama and Moses, looking."

"No scare, Ichiro!" Isaac assured. He sat on the sand letting Queenie massage his back and shoulders with coconut oil. "You know how I take care of Stanley, and why. No worries, ever, when he is with me!"

Stanley saw the struggle in his dad's expression.

"Go home now, Stanley," said Isaac. "Take a hot bath. Rub yourself down. Let your momma scold you some so her worry comes out from the inside to make her feel better."

"Ah, you Isaac!" Ichiro grinned.

Stanley took the towel his father handed him. I'm as tall as he is! he realized, jogging along beside his dad.

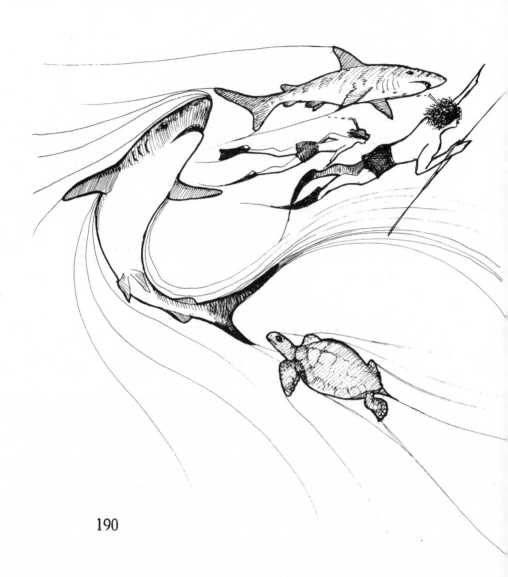

CHAPTER SEVENTEEN

There was a respite of one month in the rape of the village while the workmen cleaned and leveled the lots past the lighthouse and extended the road to them.

"Isaac, everybody but you has a lot. If you don't sign up for one, and they make you move, then what?" Stanley worried.

"Never mind! I take care. I have my plans," said Isaac. The way he spoke, with such confidence, convinced Stanley Isaac would still manage to find a way to save his place.

By the first of February, Ohta and his men were ready to move the first of the houses to the new site.

They started with Yama Ching's, jacking the

house up on blocks so the trailer could be eased underneath. The bulldozer kept "accidentally" backing into Isaac's palm trees and knocking them down one by one. Queenie stood on the verandah scolding at Isaac who stood watching in furious silence. "They knock down our house, next, if they like to!" shouted Queenie. "You sign that paper Isaac or you ruin us! You sign or I will!"

Isaac turned his back on her, shook his fist at the bulldozer, and came up to where Stanley was watching, putting off until the last minute getting aboard the school bus. Mr. Kainoa was loathe to leave this morning himself. They were going to be late.

"He mailed more letters today," said Ichiro when Stanley came home in the afternoon. "Isaac filled our mail sack. To the Board of Supervisors. To Kaumanua. To the Board of Directors of the Hawaiian Civic Club. To the newspapers. To the congressmen and both senators—airmail special delivery to Washington, D.C.!"

"He's gone out now?" Stanley asked.

"Early today," his dad answered. The black canoe was missing from the line on the beach. Every evening lately, Isaac went out and stayed until dawn. No motor, only his sail.

Isaac surprised them the next morning while they were eating breakfast.

192

"Another week and you won't recognize this place!" boasted Ohta. Isaac stood behind him, his eyes piercing the foreman's skinny body. "Going to give Waikiki some competition from here!" Ohta looked proudly down at the scars of palm trunks and the exposed green barricade of the kiawe trees, the Ching house gone and the Ii's house jacked up on blocks.

Isaac interrupted as if the foreman did not exist and had said nothing. "Ichiro," he said. "I was thinking, all night while I was out in my canoe. Remember what you told me the first day I came up here, after you and Stanley went to the kapu place? You told me why you move to Wainalii, because you want to live different. Not like on the mainland. No more rush, rush, spend your life only to make money."

"Times change," said Ichiro, pouring himself more coffee. "Isaac. Sit down with us. Have a cup of coffee. Like old times."

"You Hawaiians," said Ohta. "No good you try to turn back the clock. Be progressive! You owe it to your kids!"

"What's progressive about you making Wainalii so ugly? What's progress for my kids to move off from the seabeach to those kiawes on the bluff?"

Archer Tompkins dunked a piece of toast in his coffee and bit off the dripping mouthful before he interrupted Isaac. "Don't you take off on Mr. Ohta now, Isaac! He's a stranger here. He don't know what you're talking about. If'n you're ever going to get a job with this outfit like I have, you better give Mr. Ohta respect. He's our boss!"

Ohta looked mollified.

"You, you're a stranger too, Archer. Don't you go tell me what to do and not in my homeplace!" said Isaac. "So, okay I give up now. I cannot stop you. Here." He handed Ichiro an envelope. "My paper. I sign for Queenie and the kids, so they have a place."

"And you. You all need a place. How sensible! I knew you'd see it!" said Ichiro.

Isaac shook his head. "You no understand, Ichiro," he said in a strange tone. "Not me. Queenie. Queenie and the kids. Stanley, you come down below a minute? Something I like to say to you alone."

Stanley got up, self-conscious with Ohta and all the workmen and his father staring at him and Isaac. He walked with Isaac down the drive. They stood in the road, out of hearing of those above.

"So, I have *hanai* you," Isaac said. "You know how I feel for you, Stanley. Like you were my own son, more close to me than my own. Secrets Queenie doesn't know, secret things I made up my mind no use to pass along before I met you—I passed those things on to you, then I told you the stories I told nobody else. I thought then it was good what I did.

194

Now, Stanley—" Isaac sighed. His eyes were wet with tears. "I did wrong, Stanley. I like apologize to you. No good that I load your mind with what is gone, and over, and done with." He gazed at Stanley in such a melancholy, disconcerting way that Stanley felt the tears sting in his own eyes. He blinked hard to keep them back, to keep himself in control. "Better you try to forget all what I told you, all what you and I did together. Don't think about such things anymore, Stanley. Clean them from your mind. Forget about them—and me." His hand was an embrace, and a farewell on Stanley's shoulder.

"No! Don't talk like this, Isaac. Never!" Stanley wiped the back of his hand across his eyes and swallowed hard.

"Aloha!" said Isaac. He turned and hurried across the road. Stanley started to follow.

"Stanley!" His father called him back. He came down, and they watched Isaac disappear into his house. "He's upset. He'll get over it. Tomorrow. Or next day. Or next week."

"No he won't." Stanley shook his head.

"He has to," said Ichiro. "What is, is. What happened, happened. Sure it's going to be different. But it will be nicer, the new Wainalii. More beautiful than before, Stanley. You wait! Isaac is foolish to feel how he does."

Stanley looked at his father without saying anything. He doesn't understand, he thought. And there was no use trying to explain.

"Come. Finish your breakfast. Get your books. You'll miss the bus," said Ichiro.

Reluctantly, Stanley went back up with his dad.

Ohta was sitting over his coffee, looking amused. "He's a character, that big Isaac Kaimana!"

The sharp sweet smell of the foreman's cigarette assailed Stanley's nostrils. He didn't like Ohta. He didn't like the way he looked, or acted, or what he said.

"He's a special kind, Isaac is," defended Ichiro.

"He's crazy, I think," said Archer Tompkins.

As slowly as he dared, Stanley went down to the road, hoping he would miss the bus. He wished the screen of the palm grove was still there so he could sneak around it without being seen. He would give anything to be able to go off with Isaac in his canoe for a sail instead of having to go to school.

His hunch was right. When he came home at four, the black canoe was gone. Ohta and his bull-dozer had eaten their way into the last of Isaac's palm trees. They had knocked down part of the stone boundary wall. Ii's house was gone. Two houses now stood up on the clifftop beyond the lighthouse in barren ugliness.

Stanley was up in the house, changing from his

196

school clothes, when the telephone rang in the store. Without electricity, there was no yellow siren mounted on a pole at Wainalii as there was in the beach areas of less remote parts of the island. Ichiro came running out of the store. "Stanley! Quick! That was Civil Defense in Hilo! Tell everybody turn on their radio. Keep listening. There's been a big earthquake in South America. They think a tidal wave might get to us—by midnight, they said!"

All the oldtimers in Wainalii took the news without excitement. "First time since you folks moved in that we had tidal wave alert?" asked Lester Ching. "I guess. That's how it goes. Sometimes every month they telephone us a warning. We pack up and go out. Nothing happens. Sometimes one year, two years even goes by and no alert. We always go out though. 1960, that was a bad one."

"Midnight?" asked Ohta. "Plenty of time to move out our equipment, yuh?"

Archer Tompkins was working full-time with the crew. "Tidal wave! Ain't them bad?"

Ohta shrugged. "Can be," he said in the same cool tone Lester Ching had used.

"I thought I never would say this," said Yama, "but I'm glad now we move our house. No worries anymore. High seas even worse than tidal wave sometimes, Stanley. One time in a Kona storm the ocean came up so rough we had water under the floor

197

boards. Ruin the engine in my jeep so I have it rebuilt!"

Ichiro kept the transistor radio on in the store. About seven in the evening, people began moving a few things out. Mrs. Alapai insisted they take her new kerosene refrigerator and leave it at Ching's for safekeeping. Ohta and his crew parked the bulldozer and trucks up on the new village site. Then they drove to the ranch village to see the movie that they had been planning to see all week. They didn't ask Archer, which made him mad. Yama came to the store to buy gasoline for his outboard. "Every tidal wave, we always take the canoes to sea. Then when a wave does come, they don't get busted up on the beach."

"Not too rough at sea when the wave comes by?" asked Stanley. He thought of Isaac out there sailing around, not knowing what the ocean was getting ready to do.

"Only when it hits the coast, a bay, or a valley, then you see and feel the tidal wave," Yama tried to explain. "At sea you don't even know one is passing by. Only like one big swell maybe passing under you unless you're so close inshore the wave drag you in and then smash you up when it sucks out. When the water goes out—auwe! That's when you better run fast for high ground!"

"If you leave *Malolo* on the beach, and there is

a wave, you may not have a boat left by morning," Ichiro warned Archer Tompkins.

"I ain't going nowhere no more in that. Not even to sea to save it," said Archer. "Only one thing I got I worry about losing. That's my rifle. You're high and dry here more than my camp, Sasaki. You keep it for me overnight?" Archer went down, and in a few minutes he was back with his rifle and his store of shells, all wrapped in plastic sacks.

Everyone seemed matter of fact about the warning. Get ready. Go when the time comes. But no big thing. Stanley was inclined to share his mother's apprehension. Every bulletin on the radio made him more uneasy. At ten, Ichiro decided Sueko and Bachan and the children should go up to park on the mountain road until any danger was past. They spread the bed of the panel truck with old quilts so Sheryl and Louise could sleep while they waited for the all clear. "I'll drive you up. Then I'll walk back to keep an eye on things. No worry with high ground like we have for our property, but I feel better all the same if you and the children aren't here."

"I can stay back too, Dad?" asked Stanley.

His mother surprised him. "Why not? He can help however you need him. And he can watch the store while you take us up the road."

Stanley lifted his sisters into the back of the truck and shut the rear doors. He watched them leave, then, flashlight in one hand and transistor radio in the other, he walked up and down locking the house, and wishing there was a door to lock in each of the new units. "Christmas Island. Rise of eight inches recorded at 10:17 P.M.," said the radio. Stanley walked with the flashlight and radio down the driveway to watch the Kaimanas leave. Queenie had the truck bed loaded with furniture, mattresses piled on top of the load, and Junior, Kimo, and Iwalani squeezed into the cab with bundles of bedding and clothes. She stopped, when she saw Stanley's light.

"Isaac still out?" Stanley asked.

"He'll stay out, too, when he sees the others coming. All the canoes went already. Anything new from the radio?"

"Eight-inch rise on Christmas Island," said Stanley. "Announcer just said."

Queenie shrugged. "Eight inches? Small wave again then. I'll be glad when we get moved off the beach. No worry for tidal wave up those new lots. Isaac is too hardheaded. This pack up every time for tidal wave alert, and move out all your things in case, and worry for your house when high seas come in— no good!"

"Stanley, you lucky! I like stay back too and watch for the wave, but my mother no like for me to!" called Junior.

"You bet I no like for you to!" said Queenie.

200

She stepped on the gas pedal. "Take care, Stanley!"

By eleven, Stanley was glad to see his father's flashlight returning along the road. Everyone had left by now. It was lonesome and eerie in the darkness waiting for twelve o'clock to come. He and his dad sat on the bench at the edge of the courtyard, listening to the radio. Within minutes after they turned off their flashlights, Stanley's eyes adjusted so that the outlines and shapes of buildings were discernible below. Funny, how it still looked ugly and naked even in the dark with the palm grove gone.

The eleven-thirty news reported Johnson Island had less of a rise than Christmas. The police in Honolulu were reported to be having trouble keeping the tourists and local sightseers off Waikiki Beach. Stanley noticed that his father had fallen asleep sitting bolt upright. He reached down and shut off the radio. He slid down and lay on his half of the bench, looking up at the Milky Way through the screen of the milo branches. He'd been up since half-past five this morning. It had been a long day at school. The darkness, the quiet, the deep intermittent rhythms of his father's snoring accentuated his own drowsiness.

Presently he dozed off. He began to dream, one of those dreams that are so vivid, so intense, that they seem to be more real than any experience directly lived. In his dream, he had played hookey this morning and gone out in the black canoe with Isaac. Now, in the dream, it was night. They were as far out as they had been that time he and Isaac had gone out in the storm. They knew, both of them, that a tidal wave was coming. The wind was blowing hard. The sail rattled as if the canvas would split. The canoe drove ahead, skimming the water, spray flinging back into Stanley's face and drenching his shoulders and back. As before, he was slightly sea-sick. As before, he was scared. Isaac kept telling him to look back at something that made Isaac happy. Finally, though in the dream his eyes seemed glued together, Stanley managed to open them. There in the darkness he could see a red shark following the canoe through the black rough windy ocean. "Him?" he asked Isaac. "Him," Isaac smiled.

The canoe wavered and plunged into a towering swell that rose out of the darkness, a swell that was a wall of water bearing down on them. A gust ripped the yellow sail, splitting it with a noise like a gun-shot. They capsized before Stanley could cry a warn-ing. He was dashed from the canoe with a force so powerful that he could see the black hull breaking into splinters.

In his dream, he was conscious and frantic as he was thrown into the water. He would drown, he was certain. He tried to call out to Isaac. He gurgled

202

and spat and choked, drowning. He grabbed for a red shape coming to help him. His hand clung and held the edge of the bench on which he was sleeping. "Eh!" he exclaimed aloud.

His consciousness jolted out of the dream with his father's hand a reality on his arm and his father's whisper warning him, "Shhhhh!"

Stanley sat up, still half in the grip of the nightmare. He was out at sea grabbing the red back of a shark. He washed up and down, up and down, tossed like a coconut in the waves. He felt queer. His arms and legs were not a part of him any longer. Or was it Isaac who was queer, who was changed and different in a frightening way. Something's happened to Isaac! Stanley thought, realizing the dream had been a dream but possessed by it even so. "Auwe!" he whispered. He rubbed his sleep-prickled face. His fingers were numb. He shook them and rubbed them.

"Shhhhh!" his father admonished.

Somebody was walking up the driveway. Somebody was groping up onto the steps of the store. Somebody was fumbling to pry the lock and slide open the glass doors.

Stanley reached for the flashlight beside him and turned it on. The beam of light caught Archer Tompkins with his hands on the lock.

Archer turned, his small eyes blinded and blinking. His face was guilty, sly. "Oh. Sasaki! I come up to borrow a flashlight off'n you. I figured you had gone to the mountain road like everybody else."

"Flashlight. What's that in your hand?" said Ichiro.

Archer Tompkins' answering grin was foolish. "I needed batteries."

Stanley stayed on the bench trying to shake himself out of the dream and out of the premonition with which the dream had left him. His father got up and opened the store. He led the way with the flashlight to the display rack where he kept batteries. "Three?"

"Two," said Archer. He unscrewed the end of the flashlight he was carrying. He dumped the batteries from it out and into his pocket. Ichiro handed him the two new ones.

"How come you keep the old ones if they're no good?"

"Well now, you would think of that, Sasaki!" said Archer. He giggled. He slid the new batteries in and screwed the cap back on the end of the flashlight.

"Works?"

"Oh. Sure." Archer turned it on, then off again. "Yeah. Thanks. Works fine."

Ichiro led him back outside, shut the store doors and refastened the lock.

204

"How come you and Stanley staying here?" Archer wanted to know. "I seen your truck go up a long time ago."

"I took my wife and my mother and the young ones up. Stanley and me, we're staying here to keep an eye on the place." He looked accusingly at Archer. "Good thing we did, I guess."

Archer laughed.

Stanley moved over and away as Archer came and sat down on the bench beside him. "You don't have no radio?"

Stanley turned the radio on again. ". . . repeat," said the announcer, "at eleven fifty-nine, the tidal wave gauge in Hilo Harbor on the Big Island registered a rise of one foot six inches."

"I told Mateo he was wasting his time. He had Yama help him move his fighting chickens up the hill even," said Archer.

"You never know," said Ichiro.

Archer got up. Stanley waited impatiently for him to leave. He did not like being around Archer Tompkins.

In a few minutes, Alapais' jeep rattled along the road. Archer ran down, hailed them, and got into their jeep. Stanley stood in the courtyard watching the headlights shine through the village. Presently a light showed in Alapais' house and a light at Ah Fook's, a light in Archer's camp. "One foot six inches. Not enough to wash up to where they keep the canoes," said Ichiro. Stanley switched stations on the radio. Honolulu. Kauai. Maui. All along the dial there was nothing more being mentioned about the tidal wave alert. Only music, advertising, more music. "That's all? That's all there's going to be to it?" he said in disbelief.

"Stanley! Don't sound disappointed!" Ichiro sighed. "Every time we have an alert and no wave comes in, we're lucky!" He reached over and turned down the volume on the radio, then turned it off. "Sounds like somebody's canoe coming in. Let's go see—" He got up and turned on his flashlight. "Isaac maybe—"

Stanley started to say something about his dream, and how sure he was they would never see Isaac or the black canoe again. Then he changed his mind. "Not Isaac," he said. "He has only his sail." He walked down to the beach alongside his father, listening to the radio music, "Green Rose Hula," slack key, from Alapais' house. On the beach, somebody was holding up a lantern for the canoe idling in across the bay. It was Mr. Pahanui. They were within ten feet of him when Stanley stopped.

"Dad!" said Stanley. "Funny sound. Listen!"

A sudden clattering noise came from the bay, like rocks rattled in an empty pail. They paused at the ridge where the canoes were kept. Pahanui's canoe was the only one there. It was Mr. Pahanui standing with his lantern. Stanley shone his flashlight past the glare of the lantern on what was, ordinarily, the surface of the bay. The light picked out, instead, wet empty sand and rocks and fish left gasping in air by the water's recession.

"Tidal wave!" screamed Mr. Pahanui.

Stanley grabbed his father's hand. They turned and ran. As they passed Alapais', they yelled, "Tidal wave!" They kept on sprinting, seeing the Alapaises run to the door and out of the house. The breath hurt in Stanley's chest as they raced along the path by the pond. They were at the road when the wave smashed upon the beach with an explosive roar. The water surged through the village behind them. They ran up their steep driveway, swirling water rushing around their ankles. Ichiro dropped the flashlight. Stanley dropped the radio. "Up!" Ichiro boosted Stanley and jumped himself. They scrambled from the tabletop in the courtyard up into the low hanging branches of the milo tree. It held them while, in the darkness, they could hear the sound of the water tearing at the glass sliding doors of the store and surging up toward the house.

"Don't be scared! Hang on!" Ichiro kept saying. He sounded terrified.

"No scare, Dad!" Stanley kept reassuring him. Odd, he thought, he wasn't scared. They were going to be all right, he and his dad. Stanley knew.

Below, the wave receded, tearing at everything in its rush out. There were grinding ripping noises. Stanley fancied he could hear calls for help. No lights on now in Alapais' or Ah Fook's. No lantern on the beach. No sign of Archer's camp. Stanley climbed up to the highest branches of the tree that would bear his weight. His father followed him.

From the bay, there was the swishing, rattling sound of loose rocks dashed against each other by the receding wave. Stanley waited, sweat pouring off him, for the sound of the second wave.

"Don't let go. No matter how long, don't let go!" Ichiro pleaded.

It was forty-five minutes, an eternity, while four more waves sucked all the water out of the bay and then piled it up and slammed it back over the village and the road, up the steep bank, into the courtyard, and against the glass front of the store. It was another forty-five minutes of agony waiting for a fifth wave. Stanley was cramped and exhausted from hanging on to the milo branch. He knew he must not move. He tried to balance his weight, crouching on one branch and holding with his hands onto a branch above, his back braced against the sturdy trunk. He was more tired than he ever remembered being, but still not afraid. The dream of early evening kept invading his mind. He kept worrying about Isaac.

"Good boy!" his father kept saying. "No worry. We're going to be okay. Everything's going to be all right!"

CHAPTER EIGHTEEN

When they dared climb down from the milo tree, the moon had risen. In its light, they explored the courtyard. It was littered with debris like a beach—dead crabs, palm fronds, coconuts, dying fish, junk. There was a silt of sand several inches deep underfoot, and a scattered rubble of small stones and pieces of broken coral. One table was caught in the bushes on the bank—otherwise the courtyard was emptied of its furniture.

They walked to the house. The water had come up to the verandah steps and washed over the sill of the doorless new units. They got a flashlight and keys for the store. Stanley shone the flashlight against the high-water mark on the washhouse. It

210

had taken away the stool that Louise and Sheryl stood on to reach the outdoor sink to brush their teeth. All the bottles of disinfectant and bleach, the cleaning rags and old sponges his mother kept underneath the sink were gone. They stepped over the wash of sand and debris to the store steps. They unlocked the doors and slid them open. Some water had forced its way underneath and stayed in puddles on the wooden floor. The glass doors were full of deep gouges at the base where the water-churned debris had scoured against them. Mr. Sasaki turned his flashlight down the slope of the drive. "You suppose—" he said. Stanley knew what his father was thinking. The cars returning as the wave struck.

"Some coming back now," said Stanley.

"Your mama . . ." His dad choked. He began running toward the cars coming along the road. The first car stopped at the signal of their flashlights. It was Mrs. Kainoa. "Sueko's coming down. She's okay. We never started back, her and me."

Mrs. Kainoa turned off toward the village lane and put on her brakes. Her headlights picked out the surface of the pond where the village had been.

"Auwe!" gasped Stanley. He buried his face against his father's shirt. It looked worse than his dream!

"Nothing," said Ichiro. "Nothing left at all." His grip tightened around Stanley, who forced himself to look a second time, and to stay looking. Nothing. Nothing at all was left of Wainalii.

Mrs. Kainoa backed up and parked the car at the foot of their driveway. She got out of the car and stood there, stunned.

"Go on up to my place," said Ichiro. "Stanley, put a lantern on in the store. And in the house." Stanley took Mrs. Kainoa by the hand. He guided her across the debris and up the incline. She sat down on the store step.

"Just let me be," she said, beginning to cry. Stanley lighted a lantern and hung it from the hook in the ceiling of the store. He went up to the house and hung lanterns in the kitchen and living room. Then he hurried back down to the road. Queenie Kaimana was parking her truck. Iwalani was asleep. Junior and Kimo were awake with solemn faces and scared eyes.

"He didn't come back?" said Queenie.

Ichiro shook his head. Only one canoe was coming in when it hit. Alapai, from what I guessed by the motor sound. Pahanui was already back."

"Isaac never take his motor with him these days," said Queenie.

Stanley looked at her, and at Junior and Kimo. How could he tell them he knew, he had been there, that he was certain Isaac had made his choice not to come back ever again. He shuddered, trying to shunt the recollection of the dream from his mind.

Queenie stared across the road at the drowned place that had been the village.

"Mama! No more house!" Junior exclaimed.

"Use our house tonight. Help yourself to whatever you need," Ichiro told her. He helped carry Iwalani up to the house. Stanley stayed at the road. "Mom!" he yelled as the truck wavered unsteadily from one side of the road to the other and stopped with a squeal of brakes behind Kainoa's. "Mom! Mom!" He grabbed the truck door open while the cab was still rocking from the brakes stopping it so fast. He threw his arms around her and hugged her. He hugged his sisters. He embraced his grandmother. He squeezed the small sleeping bundle of his baby brother. He stood by listening to his father scold his mother for driving by herself and at the same time holding her so tightly that Stanley thought he might be breaking her ribs. Both of them were weeping. Ba-chan was weeping. Sheryl and Louise began crying because everyone else was. The baby began to cry. Stanley picked him up and comforted him and carried him to his crib.

As each of the village cars returned, Stanley and his dad met them at the road. Use the house, they

213

urged each one. Use the store. Help yourselves to what you need.

After the last one was back, the two of them tried to go across the road and reconnoiter, but they were forced back. The water was waist deep. Despite the all clear on the radio, every few minutes a fresh surge sent water piling up to the edge of, and sometimes onto the road, then receding. The wave action was still powerful.

"Not safe yet. Morning time better," said Mateo. They spent what was left of the night talking in low voices in the store. Children were asleep on the floor. Up in the house all the beds and floor spaces were filled. Sueko made pots of coffee. They kept the radio on, but there was little news. Until dawn they did not mention the names of the ones who weren't there from the village. The Alapaises. Ah Fook. Archer Tompkins. Yama. Solomon Ii. Mr. Kainoa. Pahanuis. Isaac.

The ones caught by the wave—maybe a chance they had been swept out and caught hold of a floating timber. Maybe a chance yet they would be found if they could keep afloat until it grew light. Nobody dared speculate. The ones who had stayed outside the bay in canoes ought to be safe. They'd have to wait for the surge to let up and for daylight before they would try to come in.

214

Stanley listened to his father's confidence with the ugly intuitive certainty of despair. Last night's dream shared the reality of waiting out the waves in the milo tree. He kept looking at Queenie who was so matter-of-fact, expecting Isaac to sail home. I know better. I know. I saw, Stanley remembered. He thought of Isaac's parting words yesterday morning. Aloha. That had been his farewell. Remembering the part of his dream where the sharks had hovered, and what he had seen and known and knew now must be so—Stanley's bowels cramped with terror. Could not! Could not be! Only a dream, he kept trying to convince himself, but it stayed with him— the intuition, the knowledge, the image he could not reason out of his mind.

At the first gray show of light, they all went out in the courtyard to look. Nobody said anything. Some of the women wept as they had off and on all night.

Where the village had been, where houses had stood up on stilts awaiting the gooseneck trailer, where junk had been piled and pigs had rooted and roosters been staked out to practice fight—where children had played and people stretched out for daytime naps and the young girls walked, tossing their waist-length black hair, where the boys had sat around strumming ukuleles and tinkering with automobile engines—there was a lagoon, rubbish, and two dead pigs.

The ridge of sand at the edge of what had been the beach was an islet. The *Malolo* was gone. Pahanui's canoe was gone. The lighthouse still stood on the point, a palm frond caught on its roof. The old post office was no more. Only half the abandoned pier remained. That half was twisted and tilted down into the water. Isaac's kaku? Stanley wondered. Where would he be? Who would know how to fish with him?

In the opposite direction the old heiau lifted its massive loosestone walls from a hilltop, aloof, indifferent, as brooding a relic as it had always seemed. I never went there with Isaac, Stanley realized. The mission church stood roofless, windowless.

The kiawe jungle looked untouched. The remains of the stone-wall boundary was half-buried in sand and water. In the bay, the surf and surge spread patterns of foam. Outside, beyond the reef, the ocean was its ordinary gunmetal sheet of early morning. Maui floated on the horizon. The mynah birds and the doves and the cardinals flew back and forth as noisy as any morning, lamenting, scolding, calling, "Come here! Come here! Pretty! Pretty!"

"Eh!" said Junior. "No more school even! What us going do?"

Stanley joined the men in their search below.

216

They picked the shallowest route to get to the sand ridge, eyes alert for what they dreaded finding.

The two Alapai boys were the first bodies. Stanley found them.

Archer Tompkins was wedged between the kiawe trees on the other side of the stone wall, his body half-buried in the sand.

A coffeepot hung as if someone had suspended it deliberately from the end of a broken kiawe branch. A kerosene stove was deposited upright at the edge of the ridge, undamaged. A bed pillow, a single sneaker, a wicker chair with the seat torn out washed in and out at the edge of the bay.

They carried up the three bodies. Then they went back. Stanley stood scanning the surface of the sea from the sand ridge. Junior and Kimo tagged after him, silent, scared. The dozens of coconuts floating offshore looked, at first glance, like so many heads. Stanley waded in and picked up the single sneaker. It was Ah Fook's.

During the morning the surge diminished. The water slowly seeped from the new lagoon. Ohta and his crew came down and helped search for more bodies. Ohta kept making notes on a memo pad from his shirt pocket, and measuring the water depth at various places. "This is going to make a difference, the kind of hotel buildings they design on this site. Whatever information I can give them on how deep the water came and where, the big bosses are sure going to appreciate!"

If Isaac were around, thought Stanley, he would smash that foreman in the face for saying such a thing. But that was why Isaac had chosen not to be around. Nothing, not even a tidal wave, was going to stop the new, changed Wainalii that Isaac dreaded.

Toward noon, they saw the canoes heading in.

"All but Isaac—" Ichiro identified each one through his binoculars. The canoes traveled back and forth in a slow searching sweep of the debris. "I don't think they'll find anybody," said Emma Ching. "Bodies maybe. But even those the sharks are going to get first."

Sharks were the first thing Yama and Lester mentioned when Stanley helped them pull up their canoe. "Three big buggers hanging around outside there. They followed us," said Yama.

"Three?" Stanley puzzled. Who would be the third?

During the afternoon a coast guard plane flew low overhead and circled, looking. The canoes went out again, with a supply of gasoline for the motors, to search. Stanley went with Solomon Ii. They were close to Ching's canoe when Yama spotted old Ah Fook floating along on the door from his house. His visored cap was on his head. His suit jacket was buttoned neatly over his denim shirt. He was propped

218

on his guava walking stick in a sitting position. One wizened foot was bare.

Stanley kept watch for the three sharks. He could sense they were somewhere close, watching him. Three, he kept thinking. One, yes. Two, he did not like to think about it, but there it was— maybe. But three?

When they returned to shore, Yama and Lester had carried Ah Fook up to the house. When Stanley came, the women had Ah Fook in the kitchen trying to feed him rice soup and hot tea. He was complaining to them in Chinese, which no one understood. After a while, he wandered down to the store, going from person to person and pointing to his bare foot. No one could find the sneaker that had washed up on the beach. Sueko found a pair of children's sneakers that fit him. She put them on him and tied the laces in a neat bow. Ah Fook let loose a torrent of Chinese and a toothless smile. Then he tottered out of the store on the third leg of his walking stick, like a clock that had been rewound.

"Bring him back!" called Yama. "He's confused. He's trying to take his regular afternoon walk!"

Mrs. Kainoa and Emma Ching had taken over the job of laying out the bodies. They usually did this in the village anyway. By dusk, the men found Mrs. Alapai and Darwin Pahanui. Stanley helped carry his friend up. The other Pahanuis and Mr. Alapai were still missing.

"And Isaac." Stanley reminded.

"Isaac?" Queenie seemed astonished that Stanley should consider Isaac missing. "If he feels like it, he stays out there two or three days, maybe. You know, Stanley!" She shrugged. "No worry for Isaac. Nothing happens to him on the ocean."

"Suppose some time he didn't want to come back?" suggested Stanley.

His father looked at him, annoyed. "When you start talking like that, you're too tired, Stanley. Go try to get some sleep!"

It was sunset before Stanley had the chance to go off by himself as he'd been wanting to all day. There was enough confusion of children running around, and everyone eating supper, and the women trying to quiet Rosie Kainoa out of a fit of hysterics, so no one saw him hurry down the driveway, and along the road, follow the ruins of the stone wall and plunge into the kiawe trees. The wave action was no more than a strong flood tide pull at his ankles as he waded around the point.

Overhead, along the beach, above the kiawes and out over the water, the sandpipers made their last evening flights. Crabs scurried out of Stanley's way. Already, among the swashes of the slight surge, they were back digging burrows in the sand. The kapu beach was no longer a tiny crescent. It was a shingle of sand packed in a hard smooth expanse up under the kiawe trees with no trace of lava rock left exposed.

Stanley looked back at the faint press of his footprints up from the water. He looked at the walls of the old heiau looming above. This was still an isolated place. The kiawes and the sea cloistered it. Here, still, was the unique special atmosphere of the old Wainalii.

Stanley groped into the kiawes to rediscover the faint trail. It took him a while. The wave had carried big coral heads in under the trees. The sand had washed inland to the clearing's edge. The water, its force broken by the density of the low branches, had flooded the clearing and beyond. The ground was wet. There was a puddle in one low spot. The air was acrid with the odor of wet kiawe humus. In the dim red light of sunset, Stanley could see the highwater mark from the wave on the side of the stone.

He walked over to it. The wave had touched, but not moved it. The size and shape, the sharklike markings on the stone were the same. It was there and yet—different, changed. The small crevices were only something like eyes. The bulge along the back

221

was vaguely reminiscent of a shark's fin. Stanley stood staring, remembering how it had looked—and, most important difference—how it had felt before.

The stone no longer gave its eerie impression of presence. The eyes neither looked back at him nor had that illusion of recognition, of being aware. The quality Isaac called mana, the aliveness that had made Stanley run from this place with fear hustling his feet, was gone. Stanley walked up to the stone with the same feeling as, this morning, he had approached the dead body of the younger Alapai boy and again this afternoon when he had helped carry the flesh and bones and inert soggy thing that had been his friend Darwin Pahanui. This was the same, the fearful mysterious difference between life and death. Stanley touched the rough stone back and the stone head. It was only a stone now. Wherever Ohta directed his bulldozer now, however they uprooted the kiawes and changed this place, or whoever came in here looking and wondering—it made no difference. This was no longer a kapu place. It was only a clearing. The big lava boulder was a stone that might, to some imagination, have the faint resemblance to a shark.

Three of them out there—three sharks following Yama Ching's canoe. "Aaaaaaah!" Stanley understood now, who the third would be. He turned, auto-

222

matically, and stooped to walk out of the clearing. He stood, dazed, on the new beach staring at the fiery afterglow of the sunset. The old one whose mana had, until last night, been lodged in the shark-shaped lava boulder. The red shark who was Isaac's brother. Isaac.

"No. Cannot be!" Stanley protested aloud to the silent beach and the uneasy ocean. The sound of his protest was no louder, no different, from the abrupt moaning sound of one kiawe limb creaking in the stillness. Stanley jammed his fist against his mouth but there was no controlling the sobs that racked his chest and ripped from his throat. He waded, stumbling, around the point, the world a blur through the tears that scalded down his cheeks. The burden of knowing what had happened to Isaac, the burden of having found the Alapai boy and of having carried the body of Darwin was like an actual physical weight crushing him from within. He shook with paroxysms of grief, weeping for all of them—even for Archer Tompkins, whom it was impossible for anyone to hate anymore.

Somehow he found the strength to walk, and then to run back along to the park, and over the stone wall. He could not shut off his weeping even though there on the sand spit ahead of him stood his father, and Yama, and Mateo, Lester, Junior, and Moses Ii.

His father was holding Archer Tompkins' rifle and
sighting along it at something out in the bay.

Stanley looked. Three shark fins sliced the surface of the water. Was it his eyes, or the light, or his
imagination that one fin was a dark red?

"No! No!" Stanley cried out, racing to stop his
father. "Don't shoot! Let me tell you who they are!"